ROMANCE

W9-BPP-371

THE UNEXPECTED
WEDDING GIFT

THE UNEXPECTED
WEDDING GIFT

BY

CATHERINE SPENCER

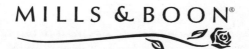

MILLS & BOON®

First published in Great Britain 2000
Large Print edition 2000
Harlequin Mills & Boon Limited,
Eton House, 18-24 Paradise Road,
Richmond, Surrey TW9 1SR

© Kathy Garner 2000

ISBN 0 263 16705 4

Set in Times Roman 16½ on 18½ pt.
16-0009-47815

Printed and bound in Great Britain
by Antony Rowe Ltd, Chippenham, Wiltshire

PROLOGUE

THE portable phone rang just as he finished
shaving. Wedging it in the angle between his
shoulder and jaw, he strapped on his watch and
headed for the bedroom. ''Ben Carreras.''

''Ben, it's Marian.''

''Hey,'' he said, checking the time. ''I'm
just about ready to leave for the airport, but I
wasn't expecting you to get here for another
hour. Did you catch an earlier flight?''

''No,'' she said, and something about the
pause that followed left the hair bristling up
the back of his neck.

''What's up, Marian? Are you okay?''

Another pause, this one, too, fraught with
some sort of tension. Then, ''I won't be coming to Vancouver tonight, after all.''

His relief left him feeling slightly ashamed
but the fact was, he'd been dreading her visit.
When she'd first mentioned flying in from

5

Calgary to spend New Year's Eve with him, he hadn't thought quickly enough to wriggle his way out of it. The truth was, though, the relationship was going nowhere and needed to be brought to an end. He'd planned to tell her so before she left.

''Gee,'' he said now, poking his finger in the drink he'd poured earlier and swirling the melting ice cube around, ''that's too bad. Did something unexpected come up?''

''In a way.'' Another pause, while she cleared her throat. ''I can't see you again. Ever.''

It was as if a load of bricks rolled off his back. Fighting to keep the elation out of his voice, he said, ''Oh? Something I did, or didn't do?''

Her sigh filtered over the long-distance connection, clear as the winter wind likely sweeping through across the prairies even as she spoke. ''No. It's just that…well, I haven't been exactly straight with you. The thing is, I'm married, Ben.''

He tightened the towel sliding low on his hips and thought it was just as well she couldn't see his grin. ''No kidding! Kind of a sudden decision, wasn't it?''

''Not really. Wayne and I have been together for three years.''

Frowning, he picked up his glass. Something here didn't compute. ''You mean, you've known him for three years.''

''No,'' she said again. ''I mean we've been married for three years.''

He paused with his drink halfway to his mouth. ''Are you telling me that all the time we've been seeing each other, you've had a husband waiting in the wings?''

''Yes.''

He swallowed a mouthful of the Scotch to try to rid himself of the sudden bad taste in his mouth. ''What took you so long to get around to telling me, Marian?''

''I'm sorry. I know I probably should have said something sooner.''

He heard the little-girl wheedling tone in her voice, like a kid hoping if she sounded cute and sorry enough, no one would notice she'd told one lie after another and finally painted herself into an impossible corner.

''There's no 'probably' about it,'' he said coldly. ''If a guy's out there gunning for me for getting it on with his wife when he's not looking, I've got a right to know.''

''It wasn't like that, Ben,'' she protested on a hiccupping little sob. ''When I met you at the beginning of October, Wayne and I were separated. I thought my marriage was over. But he's had a change of heart. He wants us to patch things up and give it another go, and so do I.''

Another semi-tearful sniffle gurgled down the line, followed by a man's voice muttering in the background like a Rottweiler getting set to square off against a poodle. The irate husband putting in his two bits' worth, no doubt!

''There's no use trying to talk me out of it,'' she said hurriedly. ''We're finished, Ben.''

Damn right, lady! The pity of it is that we ever got started.

''I'm sorry if this hurts you.''

"I'll survive," he said. *And how!* "Have a nice life, Marian. I hope things work out the way you want them to."

"Thanks," she said. "Goodbye, Ben. And happy New Year."

CHAPTER ONE

THE speeches were over, the ceremonial cutting of the cake done. During the lull in proceedings, waiters moved among the tables, refilling champagne flutes or, for those bored with Perrier Jouet, pouring two-hundred-dollar half bottles of ice wine as casually as if it were common tap water. On the dais at the far end of the ballroom, a ten-piece dance orchestra replaced the string quartet that had provided the dinner music.

If he'd been asked, Ben would have settled for a less fancy wedding. In fact, all he'd have needed to make it perfect was Julia. But he hadn't been asked. His new mother-in-law had taken charge, consulting him only when she absolutely had to, and even then not quite managing to control the grimace creeping over her patrician features at the thought of his becoming part of the family.

10

"The man's in bathrooms and kitchens, for pity's sake!" he'd once overheard her exclaim to one of her golfing cronies. "Oh, Julia can protest all she likes that he's president of his own company and there's a mile-long waiting list of clients begging to have him design for their homes, but I hardly consider being able to build a few fancy cabinets a passport to society."

"I'd give my eyeteeth to have his team work on my kitchen," the friend had replied. "Marjorie Ames brought him in to do hers and the value of her house shot up past the million-dollar mark as a result."

Unimpressed, Stephanie Montgomery had tossed her expensively permed head in contempt. "He's still nothing more than a glorified plumber, as far as I'm concerned."

But Ben didn't care what she thought of him. He had Julia; his love, his life, and now, at last and forever, his wife.

Her left hand rested on the table beside him, soft and graceful, the broad gold wedding band he'd placed on her finger not three hours before anchored behind her diamond solitaire engagement ring. The realization, again, that out of all the men she could have had, she'd chosen him—*him!*—left his throat thick with emotion. He hadn't known it was possible to love like this.

He slewed a glance her way, wanting to capture again in his mind the image of her as she was on this, their wedding day. He'd known she'd be a beautiful bride, because she was a beautiful woman in every sense of the word. Still, the sweep of her dark hair caught up in the jeweled tiara holding her veil in place, and her profile backlit by the late July sunset mirrored on the tall open windows, stole his breath away. She looked magical, an angel, so lovely he couldn't find the words to tell her how moved he was by the sight of her, or how incredibly lucky and blessed he felt to have been the one to win her heart.

From his seat two places farther down the table, Jim, his best man, leaned back and tapped him on the shoulder. ''Hey, pal, you're drooling!'' He smirked.

Ben grinned back and mouthed a reply. ''I'm allowed to. She's my wife!''

Over the band's subdued intro, the emcee, an old friend of the bride's family, hem-hemmed into the microphone and called on the groom to lead the bride in the first dance. Feeling as if his heart would burst with pride, Ben pushed back his chair and helped Julia to her feet.

 Looping the end of her train over her wrist, she took his hand, smiled up at him and followed him into the middle of the dance floor. He felt he should say something profound, something they'd both remember forty years from then. But the only words that came to mind were the mundane and clichéd, *May I have this dance, Mrs. Carreras?* And she deserved better than that; she deserved the best life had to offer. So he kept his mouth shut and contented himself by placing his right hand possessively in the small of her back and urging her close, the way only a husband had the right to do.

Her silk crinoline billowed around them, disguising the fact that her hips nestled snugly against him and, thank God and whoever designed her wedding gown, hiding his body's uncontrollable reaction to her nearness. He could well imagine her mother's horror, if she'd known; her whispered outrage. *He allowed himself to become aroused, Garry! Right there on the dance floor! He couldn't even wait until they were in the honeymoon suite before letting his animal lust get the better of him. That pervert publicly humiliated us and embarrassed our daughter on the most important day in her life!*

Except Julia wasn't embarrassed. She might have blushed a little when she realized the effect she was having on him, but that didn't prevent her from snuggling up a little closer and lowering her lashes in blatant, seductive promise of the night to come.

Blowing out a breath, Ben returned Mrs. Montgomery's unblinking gaze. *Like it or not, Stephanie, old dear, your lovely daughter's my wife now and until death us do part! How we choose to conduct our relationship is no longer any of your business.*

''Do you recognize the song they're playing?'' Julia's voice at his ear, her breath soft and sweet against the side of his neck, brought his attention back where it belonged.

'''If Ever I Should Leave You,''' he said, bending his head so that his mouth grazed hers. From the sidelines, a dozen flashbulbs exploded as the photographers captured the moment. ''Our special song. You must have chosen it.''

''Yes. Mother would have preferred a classical waltz, but I put my foot down. I wanted something that would have particular meaning for us. I love you so much, Ben.''

Emotion swept over him again, a tidal wave of such colossal proportion he hardly knew how to cope with it. They'd met during the intermission of a return engagement of *Camelot,* the previous February, and within minutes he'd decided she was the woman he was going to marry—a crazy idea, given that he wasn't the impulsive kind and all he knew about her was her name, that she had beautiful, dark brown eyes and that she stood about five eight in her high heels.

Still he hadn't let that stop him from inviting her out to lunch the next day, though he'd shown up expecting that, away from the romance and drama of the musical, she'd turn out to be no more special than any other pretty, well-dressed woman-about-town. That she was just as appealing in the light of a cold, blustery winter's day was a bonus, but it was her warmth, her intelligence and her lively interest in other people that ensnared him forever and made him determined to flatten every objection her parents threw up in their efforts to discourage the marriage.

"I'll prove myself to them," he'd promised her.

"Why?" she'd said. "I'm the one you're marrying and you don't have to prove a thing to me."

"I love you, too," he murmured now, forcing the words past the knot in his throat and knowing they didn't begin to convey the depth of his feelings for her. "There's never been anyone like you, Julia. I want to give you the whole world."

"I don't need the whole world. I only need you." She slipped her hand up his shoulder and caressed the back of his neck in long, slow strokes. "Remember the words to our song, Ben. That's exactly how I feel about you."

The impact of her touch sizzled clean down to the soles of his feet, with particularly graphic effect on his most susceptible quarters. Retaliating, he nuzzled her ear, flicked his tongue in its sweetly perfumed hollow and gloried in her muffled gasp of pleasure. "How soon can we sneak away from this shindig?"

"Not until you've done your duty and danced with my mother and the bridesmaids, and I've tossed the bouquet," she said primly. But the way she nudged against him, the gentle pressure of her thighs against his, told another story, inciting him to reckless abandonment of protocol. Waltz with his dragon of a mother-in-law when he could be making love to his wife? Fat chance!

"Keep this up and I'll disgrace both of us right now," he threatened, tightening his hold of her. "Do you know how badly I want to take you away from here and have you all to myself, Julia? Have you any idea how often, in the last five months, I've dreamed of holding you in my arms all night long?"

Her lovely eyes, so big and dark they reminded him of velvet pansies, clouded with apprehension. "What if I disappoint you?"

"You couldn't," he said, pressing a kiss to her temple. "Everything about you delights me."

"But I've never...we've never..."

"I know. But it hasn't been for lack of desire on my part. It's just that I wanted everything to be perfect. I wanted to do everything *right*. And if that sounds crazy to you—"

"It doesn't," she said, stroking his face and reaching up to kiss him full on the mouth. "It's sounds perfect to me, just the way you're perfect."

The flashbulbs exploded again, temporarily dazzling him. Blinking, he waited a moment for his vision to adjust, aware of nothing but the woman in his arms. "I'm a long way from perfect, sweetheart," he said, as the music slowed to a stop and a smattering of polite applause rippled around the room. "I've made my share of mistakes, just like any other man."

"I'll find a way to make you pay for them." Laughing, she pulled away from him. "And you can begin by dancing with Mother."

Reluctantly, he let her go. "Can I make it your grandmother, instead? Felicity's more my type and she's already admitted she likes to jive."

She pressed her forefinger to his mouth. "Behave! Amma's bad enough, without your encouraging her to be worse! As it is, she's probably going to arm wrestle all the unmarried women out of the way when I toss the bouquet. Haven't you noticed how outrageously she's flirting with every man in the place?"

"No," he said, both captivated and a little alarmed at the way she clung to her childhood name for Felicity. For all her sophistication and professional success, in many ways she was a very young twenty-three. Sometimes, he'd caught himself wondering if she was too young—for him, and for marriage—but then she'd surprise him with her maturity and he'd forget his reservations. ''I've only got eyes for you.''

''Just as well, my darling husband, otherwise I'd scratch them out!''

He loved the way she leaned against him when she said that, the intimate smile she turned on him as they walked back toward the head table. It was how he'd always imagined marriage should be: the private jokes, the exchanged glances that made words unnecessary, the silent communication of body language that said *I love you* from across a room packed with other people.

''I'll remember that,'' he said, as he handed her over to her father for the next dance, and prepared to square off with her mother.

Stephanie Montgomery perched on her chair as if it were a throne and she the reigning monarch. When she saw him making his way toward her, she lifted her head and flared her aristocratic nostrils, the way a queen might when being approached by a particularly smelly stable boy.

Refusing to let her spoil any part of such a special day, Ben did his best to live up to her impossible standards, practically bowing as he said, "May I have the honor of this dance, Stephanie?"

"I'd be delighted."

She didn't look delighted; she looked resigned, and as mightily offended as if he had horse manure clinging to his clothes.

Not deigning to accept the hand he extended, she stalked ahead of him onto the floor. Exasperated, he followed, keeping a respectful ten paces behind. "I'd like to thank you again for everything you've done to make today so memorable," he said, trotting her sedately around the floor.

"No need. You already did when you made your little speech. And I can't imagine that you'd have expected anything less than the absolute best. Julia is our only child, after all.''

''Of course.'' He cleared his throat and tried again. ''I give you my word I'll make her happy. She'll never have reason to regret marrying me.''

''Actions speak louder than words, Benjamin. Let's wait and see where things stand a year from now.''

Over her head, his glance connected with Julia's. The pride in her eyes gave him the wherewithal to put aside his urge to throttle her mother and to try, one last time, to strike some sort of truce instead. ''The renovations at the house should be finished by the time we get back from the honeymoon. I hope you and Garry'll both come to visit us, once we're settled.''

''Unlikely,'' she said. ''If you really wanted Julia to remain close to her family, you wouldn't have chosen to live practically in the United States of America. If she wants to see us, she can come to us. Our home, after all, will always be hers and our door always open to her.''

The woman should have been left out on the hillside at birth! Grinding his teeth, Ben gave in to temptation and spun her around with enough vigor to almost knock her clean out of her spindle-heeled shoes.

Punishment followed swiftly, in a way he never, in his worst nightmare, could have anticipated.

''Who is that person and why is she intruding on a private function?'' she suddenly squawked, raising her eyebrows so far they almost disappeared into her hairline. ''Is she one of your guests whom you've neglected to introduce to me?''

''No, Stephanie,'' he said, his patience at an end. ''Surprising though it might seem to you, I'm not such a boor that—''

But the reply fizzled into horrified silence as his glance latched on to the woman hovering at the double doors leading out to the foyer where he'd stood at the head of the receiving line not two hours earlier. Flaming red-gold hair caught in the light from the chandelier be-hind her, she peered at the crowd, clearly searching for someone.

He shook his head, as if doing so would bring him out of the sudden nightmare in which he found himself. This was his wedding day; a day that belonged to Julia and him and the future. His past had no place here. *She* had no place here.

In his panic, he stepped on Stephanie's foot, then compounded the sin by ditching her com-pletely. ''Just where do you think you're go-ing?'' she exclaimed, outrage lending an un-pleasantly shrill edge to her voice.

Loath though he was to give his mother-in-law any more ammunition than she thought she already had, Ben had more pressing con-cerns on his mind just then than appeasing her, the most immediate being to whisk the new-comer out of sight before Julia noticed her.

Weaving a hasty path among the guests im-peding his progress, he finally reached the doors. ''What the devil do you think you're doing here, Marian?'' he asked roughly, grab-

bing her by the elbow and hustling her across
the foyer to the private suite reserved for the
bridal party. The luggage he and Julia would
need for the honeymoon was stowed there,
along with their passports and travel tickets.
Her going-away outfit, something the color of
wild orchids, hung on a padded hanger from a
brass coat stand.

"I had to see you," Marian whimpered.
"We need to talk."

"What?" He stared at her incredulously.
"We haven't spoken in months. And in light
of our last conversation, I can't imagine there's
anything left for either of us to say."

"You'll change your mind when you hear
what I have to tell you."

"Marian," he said, hurriedly closing the
door to prevent anyone witnessing the conversation, "I got married today. You just gate-
crashed my wedding. Have you lost your
mind?"

Tears glazed her eyes. "I'm sorry. I didn't
know. When I went looking for you at the address they gave me at your old apartment, the

workmen at your new house just said you were here at a wedding. They didn't tell me it was yours.''

She sort of crumpled onto the little gilt sofa next to a full-length mirror and sniffled into a tissue she fished out of the big quilted bag slung over her shoulder. For all that he wished she were a million miles away, she made a pathetic sight and Ben couldn't help feeling sorry for her. "What happened, Marian? Didn't the reconciliation with your husband work out?''

''Sort of. But it won't last, unless you agree to help me.''

He rolled his eyes in disbelief. ''Why do I feel as if I'm speaking in foreign tongues here? I just got married! My wife is probably wondering where the devil I've disappeared to. As for the conclusions my mother-in-law's arrived at...'' He clapped a hand to his forehead. ''Hell, they don't bear thinking about!''

She glared at him through her tears. ''If you think you've got problems now, wait till you hear what I've got to say! And you can take that look off your face, Ben Carreras, because in light of the relationship we once had, the very least you owe me now is—''

` ''Don't go there, Marian,'' he advised her tersely. ''Our relationship, if it could ever have been called that in the first place, is over. It never really began.''

''You didn't feel that way when you slept with me, though, did you?''

''Are you here to blackmail me?'' he asked, his voice sliding to a dangerous whisper.

She shrank into the corner of the sofa. ''No. I wouldn't be here at all, if there was any other way out of this. But there's more at stake here than just your future or mine, Ben. There's the baby's.''

He'd spent most of his thirty-two years facing reality, knowing firsthand that even the most fleeting happiness always came with a price. Over the last five months, though, he'd grown complacent; had woken up every morning marveling that life just kept getting better.

But with Marian's last words hanging in the air like an ax waiting to fall, he knew he'd been lured into a fool's paradise. "What baby?" he asked, guessing ahead of time what her answer would be.

"Yours," she said.

Of course, it was a trick, a lie. One she was more than capable of perpetuating. After all, she'd kept a husband hidden away in the woodwork for the better part of two months.

So why was dread creeping over him like a shroud? Why did the only part of his mind still ticking along recognize that, in this instance at least, she was telling the truth?

Still, he tried to deny it. "I don't think so. If I'd gotten you pregnant, you'd have mentioned it long before now."

"I wasn't sure he was yours," she whispered, the tears she'd held in check at last running free. "He might have been Wayne's. I hoped he was."

"I don't see how there could have been any doubt, unless you were carrying on with both of us at the same time."

In a desperate attempt to ward off the nightmare web closing around him, he tossed out the remark almost glibly. But the flush that ran up her face and the guilty way she avoided his eyes stripped the black humor from his words and left them revealed for the ugly truth they were.

Stunned, he lowered himself next to her on the sofa. ''Tell me I'm wrong, Marian!''

She spread her hands helplessly and said again, ''I'm sorry!''

''For what? For cheating on your husband? For lying to me from the day we met? For telling me you'd taken care of contraception when you'd clearly done no such thing? Well, here's a news flash for you, Marian. 'Sorry' doesn't begin to cut it!'' He heard his voice, tight with anger, bouncing back from the walls and fought to bring it under control. ''Tell me this is some sort of sick joke.''

''It's no joke,'' she whimpered. ''I wish it were. All through the pregnancy, I hoped it wouldn't come to this. But the baby's yours, Ben. I know that for a fact because we just got the DNA tests back from the hospital and there's no way he could be Wayne's.''

Almost sick with anguish, Ben dropped his head into his hand. ''Assuming this isn't another lie, what is it you want from me now? Money?''

''No,'' she said. ''I want you to take the baby.''

He looked up at her, stunned. ''Take him where?''

''Home with you. I can't keep him. Wayne's willing to forgive me having an affair, but he won't be saddled with another man's child. If I want my marriage to last, I have to give up the baby. That's why I'm here. But if you don't want him either, I'll place him for adoption. I don't have any other choice, not if I want to keep my husband. And I do. He's the only man I've ever loved.''

''How can you love a man who forces you to give up your child?'' he exclaimed.

She shrugged. ''I'm not strong like you, Ben. I need someone to lean on.'' And as if that explained everything, she stood, slid the bag from her shoulder and dumped it at his feet. ''I could never cope alone with a baby.''

He looked from her to the bag, then back again. ''What's that for?''

''It's got things in it that you'll need. Diapers and formula and things like that. What did you think? That I'd stuffed the baby in it?''

''After all the other stunts you've pulled, I wouldn't put it past you.''

''I'm not completely without feelings, you know,'' she cried, flinching at the disgust he made no effort to hide. ''He's my child, too. I carried him inside me for nine months. I gave birth to him.'' She drew in a breath and there was an air of desperation about her when she continued, ''I have to do what's best for him. I have to keep him...safe.''

Safe? Given the context of the exchange, the word struck an odd, if not ominous note.

''So what's it to be, Ben?'' she said. ''Are you willing to raise him, or do I call Social Services and put him in their hands?''

CHAPTER TWO

BEFORE he could begin to sort through the chaos in his mind, let alone formulate a reply, the door opened. He heard the swish of silk and the sound of footsteps halting on the threshold. As if from a great distance, Julia's voice came to him, warm with concern and full of love. "Honey? Is everything all right?"

And following right after, in a tone rife with suspicion and censure, her mother's question, fired across the room like an arrow aimed with mortal intent. "I think you owe us an explanation, Benjamin. Who is this woman and what is so urgent about her business that you felt justified in walking out on your own wedding in order to accommodate her?"

Mutely, he turned and met Julia's gaze. Tried to tell her with his look that this was not how he'd have had things turn out; that he'd have given his right arm to have spared her the hurt and humiliation about to be heaped on her. But the ability to communicate without words, which been so easy on the dance floor, deserted him when he needed it most.

He saw inquiry on her lovely face. Curiosity. Kindness. And just enough anxiety to dim her radiance to a soft glow.

"We're waiting, Benjamin," his mother-in-law reminded him.

"Go away, Stephanie," he said. "This doesn't concern you."

"If it affects my daughter—and from the look on your face, I can only suppose it must—then it most certainly does concern me."

He felt cold all over. Cold and angry and afraid. In the space of fifteen minutes, everything had changed. All that he thought was his for the rest of time was seeping away, and he was helpless to stem the bleeding. "Julia," he said tightly, "what I must tell you is for your ears alone and I'm not about to have your mother decide otherwise. Either get her out of here, or I won't be responsible for my actions.''

''Mother?'' She turned, appealing to the woman with upturned palms. ''Please leave us alone.''

''With that creature?'' Stephanie gestured to where Marian wilted against the back of the sofa. ''Not a chance, my dear! If she stays, so do I.''

Ben's anger turned to rage at that, burning so white hot that his vision blurred and a kind of madness possessed him. He'd never been a violent man but, at that moment, two things came to him: he was capable of murder if that's what it took to protect those he loved; and he loved Julia more than life itself.

Fortunately, the door opened again to reveal Felicity Montgomery, perhaps the only person on the face of the earth able to stop Stephanie in her tracks with a single glance. ''There's a man with a baby waiting in the foyer,'' she said. ''He seems to think his wife's in here and he'd like to know if she's accomplished what she came to do.''

"I think we'd all like to know the answer to that, but no one's talking," Stephanie snapped. "Why don't you invite him to join the party, Mother Montgomery? Maybe he'll be more forthcoming."

But Felicity had learned a thing or two in her seventy-nine years. She didn't need anyone to spell it out for her to pick up on the hostility and tension muddying the air. "I think not, Stephanie," she said. "Ben, you look troubled. Is there anything I can do?"

"Yes," he said. "Get Julia's mother out of here before I wring her interfering neck!"

"Consider it done, dear boy," she replied serenely, taking a firm hold of his mother-in-law's elbow and steering her toward the door. "Come along, Stephanie. You heard the man."

The silence they left behind was almost worse than the belligerence that had preceded it. It spread over the room like poisonous gas, paralyzing the three remaining occupants. It seemed to Ben that the space separating him from Julia was too vast for him ever to find his way back to her.

Marian was the first to speak. ''Do you want me to wait outside, as well, Ben?''

He nodded, too full of pain to trust his voice.

Leaving the bag where she'd dropped it, she made her way to the door, hesitating only when she reached Julia. ''I'm very sorry to spoil your wedding,'' she said. ''I hope you'll believe me when I say that was never my intention.''

''Leave it, Marian!'' he barked, the thought of Julia hearing the news from anyone other than him restoring his powers of speech in a hurry.

Throughout the exchange, Julia remained motionless, her solemn gaze never once wavering from his face. ''Would you like to sit down?'' he asked, when they were finally alone.

''No,'' she said. ''I'd like you to tell me who that woman is and why she came here looking for you. And I'd like to know why she thinks she's ruined our wedding day.''

The seconds ticked by as he searched for a way to soften the blow he had to administer, but no matter how he wished it could have been otherwise, in the end a swift, sharp thrust of the sword was the most merciful. ''She claims she's the mother of my child, Julia.''

The room tilted and, for a moment, she feared she was going to pass out. *Too much excitement,* she told herself. *Too much champagne. I'm imagining all this.*

Blindly, she reached behind her, fumbling for something—anything—against which to support herself. Her hand closed over the doorknob and she squeezed it hard, hoping it would disintegrate into thin air and prove she was dreaming.

Instead, it pressed against her palm, cool and smooth and hard as glass. So hard and unforgiving that it pinched her wedding ring against the pad of flesh on her finger. Swallowing painfully, she asked the only question that mattered. ''And is she telling the truth?''

''She might very well be, yes.''

''How long have you known?''

''I just found out.''

''I see.''

But she didn't, not at all. Pressing her lips together, she let go of the doorknob and folded both hands in front of her, knowing he was watching every shift in her expression, knowing he was waiting for her to give him some sort of sign that she understood what he'd said.

She couldn't do that. Her mind was empty, a great barren void. The pity of it was that her heart didn't follow suit, because the ache in her chest was crushing the life out of her.

''Julia,'' he finally begged, ''say something, for God's sake! Give me hell. Tell me I'm the world's biggest jerk. Scream at me, if it'll help. But please don't just stand there like a wounded deer waiting for another bullet to put an end to your misery! You have to know it's killing me to do this to you, today of all days.''

''What's her name?'' she said.

He flung up his hand. ''What does it matter?''

''I'd like to know.''

''Marian,'' he said harshly. ''Marian Dawes.''

But he hadn't always felt like that, spitting out the name as if he couldn't bear the taste of it…or of her. When he'd made love to her, he'd have murmured the word, called her sweetheart, and honey, darling—all the endearments Julia thought he'd reserved especially for her.

With a little cry, she collapsed on the floor, crippled with the pain of it all. In a flash, he was at her side. She saw his hands, strong and tanned and capable, reaching for her. And in her mind's eye, she saw them touching another woman, in places he'd never touched her.

''Julia…sweetheart!''

''Don't,'' she cried, when he went to lift her, but he swept her up anyway and carrying her over to the sofa, sat down and cradled her next to his heart.

The ridiculous, overblown skirt of her wedding dress flipped up like a saucer, so that anyone walking into the room would have seen nothing but her white satin pumps and white lace stockings, and the silly blue satin garter he was supposed to throw over his shoulder to all the single men attending the wedding.

"Julia, I love you," he said. "No matter what else you might be thinking, please believe that."

She forced her next question past the aching lump in her throat. "Did you love her, too?"

He shook his head and she thought perhaps his mouth trembled a little before he managed to say, "No. Not for a moment. I've never loved anyone but you, Julia."

"But you made a *baby* with her." Once again, the images flashed through her mind: the naked intimacy that had to have taken place; the fact that, even if he'd never loved Marian Dawes, he'd still managed to...!

Had it happened in his apartment, in the bed he'd so steadfastly refused to let his fiancée ever lie in? Or in a cheap motel, on some dark country road?

Oh, she couldn't bear any of it! ''Let go of me,'' she croaked, struggling to free herself and inching as far away from him as she could get in the tiny room. ''I don't want you touching me—not after you've touched her!''

He wiped his hand over his face, and she had to look away because she found the weariness and grief in his eyes too dangerously moving. ''What do you want me to say? I'm a man, not a god. I made a mistake. I was a damn fool. It's all true, Julia, but it doesn't change the fact that I apparently have a son.'' He sighed. ''And there's more. His mother doesn't want him.''

The heaviness in his voice filled her with foreboding. ''What else are you trying to tell me, Ben?''

''She wants me to take him. And if I refuse, she'll put him up for adoption.''

''I don't believe you! What kind of mother could do that?''

''The kind whose husband won't accept the child that resulted from an extramarital affair.''

Extramarital affair? Dear lord, was the horror never going to end? Distraught beyond anything she'd ever experienced before, Julia pressed her fingers to her mouth for a moment to stop herself from crying out loud. ''So what did you tell this paragon of feminine virtue?'' she asked, resorting to sarcasm when she was able to speak because only by fueling her sense of outrage could she keep herself together, and she'd rather be dead than let him see how he'd devastated her.

''You and your mother showed up before I gave her my answer.''

His reply was so evasive, so unlike him, that her next question was redundant. Still, she had to ask, even though having her suspicions confirmed would merely tighten the strands of misery threatening to choke her. ''What would you have said, if we hadn't been so inconveniently interrupted?''

''You know the answer, Julia. I'll take him, of course.''

So there it was, the coup de grâce. Less than twenty feet away, over two hundred guests were waiting for the bride and groom to show up and go through the final hoopla associated with wedding receptions. She was expected to radiate happiness. To toss her bouquet blithely over her shoulder. To gaze adoringly at her groom, and ride off with him into the sunset in the certain belief that the happy-ever-after, which surely every bride had the right to expect, was hers for the taking.

And instead, her brand-new husband had smashed her dreams and left her with one of only two choices: she could go along with his proposed actions, or she could leave him and file for a divorce.

A sour aftertaste filled her mouth. No, not a divorce. A marriage had to be consummated before that became necessary. So a quick and easy annulment would do the job, and just like that, the marriage would be over before it had really begun.

"Have you once thought of what this means to us?" she asked him bitterly. "Of how it affects our marriage?"

"It's *all* I can think of, Julia."

"Oh, I doubt that! You've managed to think ahead to the point that you've decided to assume responsibility for a child without even knowing for sure if you're his father. You've managed to reduce our wedding day to a fiasco. You've betrayed me and everything we've planned together. But not once have you asked my opinion about what you should do next. The word 'we' hasn't once entered the conversation."

"All right, I'm asking you now," he said, his blue eyes so empty and cold that she shivered. "What would you have me do? Tell Marian to take her problems somewhere else?"

"Would you, if I asked you to?"

"No," he said flatly. "That's not who I am, Julia. I don't walk away from trouble, and I don't turn my back on helpless babies. I thought you knew me better than that."

"So did I," she said. "Obviously, I was wrong. I didn't take you for the kind of man who'd have an affair with a married woman."

"I didn't know she was married at the time."

"But you knew enough to sleep with her. To make a baby with her."

He rolled his eyes wearily. "Guilty on both counts. Sometimes, a man's brain lies below his waist—especially when a woman makes a determined play for him."

At that, the tears she'd fought to repress flooded her eyes. "I made a play for you," she said brokenly. "I practically got down on my knees and begged you to make love to me. I might not have had your old flame's experience and expertise to back me up, but I didn't just fall off the turnip cart, either. I've read books. I've seen movies where a man and a woman make love. I know the mood has to be right, and I did everything I knew how, to make it right for you. But you somehow managed to keep your brain and—" she glared at his fly "—your...*other thing* separate. How come you never got them mixed up when I tried to turn up the heat?"

"Because I love you," he said. "I love you enough to let you go, if what you've just learned leaves you too disappointed in me to give our marriage a chance to survive."

"But not enough to choose me over some other woman's child!" Oh, she hated herself for saying that, for being so selfish that she'd punish an innocent baby for his father's crimes! And she hated Ben for bringing out the worst in her. She had not known she could be so small, so mean-spirited.

"Would you still want me, if I did?"

"I don't know," she said. "I don't feel as if I know you at all. You aren't the man I fell in love with."

"Yes, I am, Julia. I'm just not perfect, and neither is life. And if you thought being married to me was going to be one long bed of roses—"

"I didn't!" she insisted, furious that he was trying to put her on the defensive. "I'm not a child. Every marriage goes through its rough spots. But I hadn't expected ours would be fighting for survival within hours of our exchanging wedding vows. When I promised to love you, for better and for worse, I...never thought...!''

The sobs rose up, choking her into silence.

''Neither did I,'' he said softly. ''And I admit this is about as bad as it can get. I admit what I'm asking of you is unfair. So the next move is up to you. Do you want me to go next door and tell everyone to go home because we've decided to call it quits? Or will you stand by me and give us a chance to prove to all those naysayers lined up behind your parents that we're up to whatever challenge life throws at us?''

He was a dirty fighter, bringing her parents into things like that! He knew her pride would never allow her to prove they'd been right when they'd said that marrying a man she'd known less than six months was rushing headlong into disaster.

But was pride enough to keep their marriage afloat? Because that was about all she had to fall back on. Oh, if she looked honestly into her heart, she knew she loved him still. But what use was love without trust, and how could she ever trust him again?

As if she weren't beleaguered enough, the door flew open behind her and a man barged into the room. From his opening salvo, she could only suppose he must be Marian Dawes's husband.

"We've hung around long enough, Carreras!" he fairly bellowed. "Make up your mind. Are you taking the kid or not?"

Marian, her face pale and drawn, hovered behind him, a tiny bundle clutched in her arms. Even Julia, drowning though she was in her own misery, couldn't help feeling sorry for what the woman must be going through. To have to choose between her child and this brute of a man—how could he ask this of her?

"I'll take him," Ben said, at which Marian let out a sigh, walked over and handed the child to him.

Julia could hardly bear to watch as Ben looked at the baby. Awkwardly, he reached out a finger and pushed aside the blanket covering its face. She heard his indrawn breath, saw the startled expression in his eyes and knew in an instant that, even if she had been his first love, she was no longer his only love. There was recognition in the gaze he turned on that little face, and wonder, and the primitive determination to protect that only a parent can know—all those things she'd expected he'd never experience until he held *their* firstborn in his arms.

A hand closed over her shoulder, and she turned to find her grandmother at her side. The compassion in Felicity's eyes undid her. Lips trembling, Julia reached up and clung to her. ''Tell me what to do, Amma, please!''

''It's not my place to say, my angel. You're facing a hard decision and it's likely only the first of many. But whatever you decide, Ben is your husband, and I'd ask you not to forget that.''

''This isn't fair!'' she wept.

''No, it's not.''

''I hurt so much.'' She pressed a fist to her chest. ''How could he break my heart like this?''

"His own heart's breaking, too, Julia. One only has to look at him to see that."

She slewed a glance his way, hoping he wouldn't notice, and found her gaze locking with his. The naked pleading in his eyes could have melted stone.

She was only vaguely aware of Marian Dawes and her husband leaving, of the sudden blast of music from the reception as the doors leading to the ballroom swung open, of her grandmother urging her forward. All her attention was fastened on the man she'd married.

The sight of him drew her like a magnet. Even at that late date, she was still hoping for a miracle, for someone to leap out from behind the curtains and shout, "Hey, this is all a big mistake. Some other guy's the father. Go back to your wedding and the lovely life you planned. This isn't your problem."

But when she finally drew abreast of Ben and looked down at the baby he held awkwardly on the palms of his hands as if it were a tray of food, her heart plummeted. Because any hope she'd entertained that he might not be Ben's son was instantly dispelled. He was a miniature carbon copy of her husband.

Numbly, she stared at the thick dark hair, the olive complexion, the brilliant blue eyes, and accepted the inevitable. Only Ben could have fathered this child.

''Your father is out of patience, Julia,'' she heard her mother exclaim from the doorway, ''and I am frankly mortified at your behavior.'' Then, as Felicity murmured a protest, ''No, Mother Montgomery, I won't be put off again! Surely even you cannot dispute that, as mother of the bride, I have the right to know why Julia and this man she's married have chosen to abandon the guests who've come here today to help them celebrate their wedding.''

''I'm afraid your mother's right,'' Felicity said.

Slowly, Julia raised her eyes and again met Ben's anguished gaze. ''Yes,'' she said. ''Amma, will you stay with...will you stay here until we come back?''

''Of course. Here, Ben, give the baby to me.''

"Ba...by?" The way her mother's outraged shriek sank to a horrified whisper would have struck Julia as comical in any other circumstances. As it was, she could only be grateful that, in Stephanie Montgomery's book of social etiquette, keeping up appearances ranked above all else.

"That's right, Mother," she said, hooking her train over her arm and sweeping toward the door with as much dignity as she could muster. "What else would you expect to find wearing a diaper and wrapped in a receiving blanket? A stuffed turkey?"

How he and Julia made it through the next hour, he didn't know, because even a moron could have cottoned on to the fact that, between the first dance and their final exit in a shower of confetti and rose petals, something had gone terribly wrong between the happy couple.

The bride refused to make eye contact with the groom and tossed her bouquet as if she were heaving a live grenade into enemy lines.

The smile stretched over her mother's mouth more accurately resembled the rictus of a woman in extremis, while the expression on her father's face would have stopped traffic. But if any of those well-dressed, well-bred, upper-echelon society guests happened to notice, no one was crass enough to remark on it.

Of course, the honeymoon plans had to be scratched. Instead of changing their clothes and heading for the airport, he and Julia climbed into the limousine in all their wedding finery and directed the driver around to the back of the country club where Felicity waited with the baby. The switch took place with furtive, undignified haste. Fortunately, the black-tinted windows in the vehicle hid the infant carrier strapped to one of the rear seats as the car sped down the driveway and headed south to White Rock.

Frequently, as they crossed the city, Ben began to speak. But one glance at Julia's profile, and the words, inadequate at best, dried up completely. She sat as if made of stone, blind and deaf to everything around her, especially the man and child sharing the back of the limousine with her.

When they were only a few minutes short of their destination, he made a last attempt to reach her. ''I love you, Julia. I need you. Please try to hold on to that. No matter how bad things seem, if you'll believe in me, in my love, we can win this. We can make it.''

''The baby's crying,'' she said.

Astonished, he looked over at the little scrap of life that was his son and saw movement beneath the blanket, heard a mewing that sounded more like a kitten in distress than a human being. What was he supposed to do? He knew next to nothing about babies except that they needed attention at both ends rather often, yet it seemed to him that removing the child from the safety of the baby carrier wasn't smart. What if the car swerved suddenly, or slammed to a stop? What if he dropped the baby on its head?

''I guess whatever's bothering him can wait,'' he muttered. ''We'll be at the house in another five minutes or so.''

She tilted her head, as though to say, *Suit yourself. He's your son,* and continued to stare unblinkingly at the back of the driver's head.

By the time they finally drew up outside the house, the mewing had escalated into an irate squawk. Leaving him to deal with that as he saw fit, Julia stepped out of the car and stalked to the front door. The driver followed with their luggage. Ben brought up the rear with the baby shrieking at the top of his tiny lungs.

''How do I make him stop?'' he asked, once they were inside.

''Don't ask me,'' Julia said. ''I've never had a baby. But I'd imagine whatever's in the bag your lady friend left with you might provide some answers.''

''She's not my lady friend, Julia,'' he said edgily.

''Your former lover, then.'' Turning to the mirror hanging above the hall table, she ripped off her wedding veil and tiara. ''It's been a long, not to mention devastating day, and I'm tired. I'll take one of the guest rooms and leave the master suite for you, since you'll be requiring extra space.''

''Julia—!'' he began. But he was drowned out by the baby's crying and even if he hadn't been, she wasn't interested in listening to anything he had to say. Deftly hoisting her skirt over her arm, she disappeared up the stairs.

He couldn't blame her. Outwardly, he might appear to be functioning on all eight cylinders but inside he was a mess. How she must be feeling he could only begin to imagine. And the devil of it was, he couldn't make consoling her his first priority.

Picking up the baby, he tried to soothe it by propping it against his chest. Its head flopped forward as if it hadn't been properly connected to the neck. The hand he'd placed under its little rear end felt suddenly wet and clammy. Something smelled.

''Cripes!'' he muttered as some sort of drool bubbled down the front of his shirt. ''You'd better have come with a book of instructions, kiddo, or you and I are in for a rough ride.''

CHAPTER THREE

THE house had five bedrooms. Julia chose one at the other end of the upstairs hall, as far away from the master suite as possible. Fortunately, the renovations had almost been completed and although the furnishings were minimal, they'd do. Anything was better than being in the same room with Ben and the baby. *That* she could not have endured. She'd have slept in the garage first.

The room smelled of fresh paint and lemon oil. There were no pictures on the walls, no knickknacks on the dresser, no reading lamps, nor even sheets on the bed. The windows were bare and the only light came from an antique brass fixture in the middle of the ceiling.

It showed her stark reflection in the mirror on the wardrobe door. She looked like the bride of Frankenstein—wild-eyed and as white as her wedding dress.

Almost everything about the wedding had been white—the flowers, the cake, the limousines. Even her bridesmaids had worn white. It had been her mother's idea. "Why not?" she'd said, when Julia had questioned the need for quite such an extreme fashion statement. "It's not only chic, it's a proclamation of your innocence. You're entitled to be married in white, unlike most brides in this day and age. Call me old-fashioned if you will, but to my way of thinking, women who've behaved like alley cats before marriage have no business parading down the aisle and trying to pass themselves off as virgins when they finally decide to settle down with one man."

Just as well Ben had worn black. At least it matched his morals.

A sob caught Julia off guard and as another wave of misery overtook her, she tugged frantically at her dress. She could not bear its smothering softness a moment longer. She heard the pop of tiny buttons pulled roughly free, the tear of fine silk. Heard the ping of hand-sewn seed pearls and crystal bugle beads rolling across the polished oak floor. And didn't care. The dress and everything it signified were a farce.

"Julia?" Ben's voice, right outside the door, had her swallowing her sobs. "May I come in?"

And witness her standing there in nothing but her stockings and the strapless merry widow that showed more of her breasts than it concealed? With her hair standing on end and her face streaked with mascara and her eyes all puffy and red from crying? "You may not!"

"I've brought up your overnight bag. I figure you'll be needing it."

"Leave it outside the door."

She heard his sigh, loaded with frustration and even a hint of annoyance. As if *she* was the one who'd ruined everything! "Have it your way."

I wish I could, she thought, listening to his footsteps fade down the hall. *If I had my way...*

But what was the use in thinking along those lines? In a few weeks' time, she'd turn twenty-four. She'd stopped believing in fairy god-mothers years ago. No one was going to come along and change things back to the way they'd been yesterday. Nothing was ever going to be the same again.

How could she and Ben possibly make their marriage work when the trust she'd believed in so completely was based on a myth? Her mother was right: she didn't know him. The outward trappings might not have changed. He was still six feet, three inches tall. His eyes were still blue, his smile as heart-stoppingly sexy as ever. But inside, where it counted, he was a stranger.

She'd thought she knew everything about him. They'd spent hours, days, exchanging life histories. She knew he'd inherited his black hair and olive skin from his Texas born Spanish-American father, but that his blue eyes and rangy height came from his Canadian mother's Norwegian ancestry.

She knew he'd been born on a train stranded halfway across the Canadian prairies in a January blizzard; that his parents had left Texas and come back to his mother's homeland to start a new life on a farm in northern Saskatchewan, left to her by an uncle she never knew.

"Trouble was," he'd told Julia, lying stretched out on the floor in front of the fireplace in his apartment, with his head in her lap, "they hadn't the first idea what they were taking on. They thought they were coming to a pretty log cabin beside a lake ringed by majestic evergreens. What they got was a tarpaper shack with an outdoor privy, a well whose pump should have been retired years earlier, the closest body of water a slough frozen solid eight months of the year, and summers plagued with mosquitoes and black flies."

"But they were happy," she'd said hopefully, because she found their story so touchingly romantic.

''Hardly! They had no concept of the bone-cracking, deep-freezing cold of the Canadian north, and no idea at all how to work a farm, which is a tough undertaking even for people born to the life. We survived those early years only through the generosity and pity of neighbors who came to our rescue an embarrassing number of times.''

''But, in the end, they made a go of things?''

''In the end, they lost everything, including their lives. I was ten at the time, and winter was particularly vicious that year. To try to keep the house warm, my clueless father overloaded the woodstove and burned the place to the ground. The neighbors came running—again—but there was nothing anyone could do. The place went up like a rocket.''

He'd swung himself to a sitting position and hunched forward over his knees so that she couldn't see his face, and his voice had been hoarse with emotion when he'd continued, ''I'd been sent out to bring in more wood, and I'll never forget the noise or the heat as that pathetic shack literally exploded into a ball of fire, or the hiss of sparks landing on frozen snow.'' He'd drawn in a long, shuddering breath. ''Or the screams of my parents trapped inside.''

Julia had wrapped her arms around him and warmed the back of his neck with her tears. ''Oh, Ben!'' she'd murmured brokenly. ''I'm so sorry.''

He'd shaken his head, impatient with himself and with those poor people who hadn't lived long enough to see what a fine man their son had become. ''My mother's dreams of happy-ever-after were slapped down time and again by my father's inability to provide for his family. He was a dreamer, a poet, as unsuited to that corner of the world as a palm tree is to an iceberg, and unwilling to adapt. Yet she loved him regardless and would have been lost without him. It was just as well they both went together.''

''But what about you? You were just a child. Who took care of you?''

''The same people who'd taken care of us all from the day we set foot in the area. For the next six years, I was passed around from one family to another, depending on who had a bed to spare and who could afford to feed another mouth.''

''Weren't there any relatives who could have taken you in?''

''No. And it was a matter of pride in that kind of tight-knit group for people to look after their own, without interference from government agencies or the like.''

Desperate to find some sort of silver lining to the story, she'd stroked his hair and murmured, ''But that was good, wasn't it? Better than being sent away to live with strangers?''

''I guess. But for all that those good people tried, I never fit into their stalwart Norwegian community. Blue eyes and lanky height notwithstanding, I was as much an alien as if I'd landed from Mars, marked with my father's genes and because of my resemblance to him, tarred with the same brush of incompetence. No matter how hard I tried, whether it was working from dawn to dusk on the land or scoring the winning goal for the local ice hockey team, I was still the son of that impractical fool Carreras, who'd been too busy writing rhyming couplets about the northern lights to learn the rudiments of survival.''

He'd turned around and looked at her long and seriously then. ''I dropped out of school when I was sixteen, Julia. One day, I left Saskatchewan on a Greyhound bus, bound for wherever I could get for the price of the ticket I could afford, and ended up in Vancouver. I don't come from old money, with a university education and enough influential relatives to ensure my automatic entry to the best clubs. Sure, I'm CEO of my own company, but I seldom wear a business suit and until recently, I didn't drive a fancy car. So I understand why your folks think I'm not good enough for you. But I promise you this. I'll never let my wife go short of anything—not food, or shelter, or decent living conditions. If I have to work the clock around, seven days a week, to provide a good life for my family, I will. I'll prove myself worthy of you and I swear I'll never give you reason to regret marrying me.''

He'd spoken with such heartfelt sincerity but words, she now realized, were cheap when they weren't backed up by actions. Before she'd had time to grow used to the feel of his wedding ring on her finger, he'd broken his most sacred promises. How could he have done that, if he loved her the way he claimed he did?

Weary from going over the same ground time and again, but too strung up to sleep, she turned off the light and opened the window. The night sky was so clear that she could see all the way to Washington State and the ghostly shape of Mount Baker, snow-covered year round, riding the horizon to the east. To the southwest, the waters of Semiahmoo Bay lapped quietly against the shore.

The scent of roses drifted on the warm air, and night-scented stocks. There was a sliver of moon casting a rippled path of light over the sea. If she leaned out far enough, she could just catch the glimmer of lights from the sidewalk restaurants lining Marine Drive. There'd be music and laughter down there; the clink of wineglasses, the flickering glow of candles throwing shadows over the flowers spilling from the planters and hanging baskets outside each establishment.

It was a night made for lovers, for honeymooners; for lying beside one's new husband in the moon-splashed darkness and discovering what true intimacy was all about. But she had never felt more alone. Ben was only a few yards away, yet the distance between them was such that he might as well have been on the other side of the world.

Thinking about it, about him, brought the disappointment and hurt surging back with a vengeance, enough that it might have overwhelmed her all over again if another sound hadn't penetrated the quiet.

She stopped in the act of turning away from the window and listened. It came again, from somewhere in the house, the thin heart-rending wail of a very new baby. Ben's baby.

She didn't want to hear it. Didn't want to know why it was crying. But nor could she ignore it. An only child herself, she hadn't been exposed to infants. Her experience with them was so slight, it was negligible. Yet she knew instinctively that the poor little mite was missing its mother and she couldn't bear it.

Turning on the light again, she rummaged through her overnight case for something with which to cover herself since she had no intention of venturing forth in her undergarments. The only item she found was the satin nightgown and matching peignoir—white, of course—that had been a trousseau gift from her mother. It was a lovely thing, lavishly embroidered with lace inserts, too frivolous and romantic by far for the present situation, but it would have to serve.

The upper floor was in darkness when she stepped into the hall but there was light showing below. Silently, she made her way to the top of the staircase, not daring to think too far ahead, not knowing if she could do anything to soothe the baby, knowing only that she could not ignore its pitiful cries.

She was halfway down the stairs when a stream of light from the kitchen flooded into the lower hall. A moment later, she froze as Ben appeared.

He'd removed his dinner jacket, left his bow tie hanging loose around his neck and had undone the top button of his dress shirt. He had a tea towel slung over his shoulder and was holding the baby as if it were a football, resting its head against the fingertips of his right hand and its little bottom on his palm of his left hand, with its legs tucked into the crook of his elbow.

He was humming to the child and jiggling it much too energetically. Her heart jumped with fear as he negotiated the newel post at the foot of the stairs. Another inch or two to the right, and he'd have banged the baby's head.

Be careful! she wanted to cry out. *Watch where you're going and don't toss him around like that unless you want him to get sick to his little stomach. Hold him so that he can hear your heart beat, not as if you're about to try for a touchdown!*

Perhaps she made a sound, or perhaps she moved because Ben suddenly stopped in his tracks and glanced up, trapping her as she hovered with one foot extended toward the next stair. She wanted to look away, to run back the way she'd come, but he would not release her from his gaze.

The seconds spun out, marked by the quiet tick of the Vienna clock hanging opposite the front door. At length, Ben said, ''He threw up all over me but he's asleep finally.''

She nodded, unable to speak for the enormous lump in her throat. There was a huskiness in his voice, a touching tenderness in his eyes as he glanced briefly at the child, and she knew that the emotion that had crossed his face when he first held his son had intensified in the hours since. He was irrevocably in love with his baby. He would never be all hers, ever again.

''Were you looking for me, Julia?'' he asked, coming up to where she waited.

''No.'' The answer emerged in a rusty whisper.

''Is there something you'd like?'' He lifted his shoulders in a shrug, a slight movement only but enough to stir the baby to a squawk of sleepy indignation. ''The refrigerator's empty so I can't offer you hot milk, but there's brandy in the liquor cabinet if you need something to help you sleep.''

An ocean of brandy couldn't put her to sleep! And even if it could, did he really think a good night's rest would do the trick and she'd feel better about everything in the morning?

The resentment that had alternately seethed and simmered within her from the minute her wedding day had collapsed in ruins flared to new life again. ''There's not a thing you can do for me!'' she spat, tossing the words over her shoulder as she fled back to her room with her peignoir swirling around her ankles like mist.

He fell asleep just after midnight, only to have the baby waken him about an hour later.

Wiping the grit out of his eyes, he scooped the child out of the drawer he'd set up as a make-shift crib and lay it on the bed so that he could change its soggy rear end.

It was a chore that took some getting used to. No matter how careful he was or which part he tackled first, something always managed to leak or fall out of the diaper he removed before he could juggle a clean one in place.

To add to the problem, the baby seemed to know he was in the hands of a novice. The minute his backside was exposed, he set up a wriggling that would have done an eel proud.

As for being able to squirt...! His deadly aim and ever-ready supply of ammunition was nothing short of amazing for someone so small!

"Bear with me, kiddo," Ben muttered, fumbling to secure the diaper's adhesive tabs in place as the infant set up an outraged howling accompanied by a frenzy of kicking. "I'll look after the other end as soon as I'm done down here."

He assumed that's what all this to-do was about: that the child was hungry again. But hell, what did he know? The closest he'd ever come to a baby before tonight was when he'd still been living in Saskatchewan and the woman who'd taken him in gave birth to twins. Two days later, he'd been shunted over to the neighboring farm, to make room for the new arrivals.

"Hang in, Squirt," he begged, stuffing the skinny little legs back into the one-piece sleeper—a near impossible task, since the minute he got one foot in place, the other flipped free again. "I'll get that bottle to you ASAP."

He could use a bottle himself—preferably one full of Jack Daniels. With a straw stuck in the neck!

Cradling the child to his chest, he went down to the kitchen refrigerator and pulled out one of the bottles of formula he'd found stashed in the bag Marian had left with him. "Here," he said, popping the rubber nipple into the baby's mouth.

A moment of blessed silence reigned then splat! Formula dribbling out of the corners of its mouth, the kid rejected the bottle and filled the night with another shriek of rage.

Helplessly, Ben stared at the pint-size tyrant in his arms. "Well, what *do* you want then?"

Practically blue in the face with fury, the baby screamed back at him. Seizing opportunity while he had the chance, Ben again stuffed the nipple back in the wide open mouth, then hurriedly withdrew it as the baby dissolved into a paroxysm of choking.

"Shee-oot!" he cursed, and rocked the tiny body frantically. "I need help. Now!"

Somebody heard him. Not God, whom he'd meant to call on, but Julia. She appeared from the shadows, modestly clutching the filmy dressing gown thing—a negligee he supposed it was called—over her low-cut nightgown. Her dark hair flowed loose about her face and he thought she was the most beautiful creature he'd ever set eyes on. "Hey," he said, raising his voice over the baby's din. "Did we wake you?"

Oh, brother, talk about a dumb question! Half the neighborhood was probably awake by now.

"I wasn't sleeping," she said.

He grinned weakly. "We aren't having the best night, either."

Her glance veered toward the baby, then slid quickly away again. "He sounds upset."

Just in case anyone felt like arguing the point, the kid set up a fresh howling. With his eyes scrunched shut and his mouth all twisted to one side, he looked, Ben thought, like a wrinkled, dried-up apple carved to resemble an old woman.

"I thought he was hungry but he won't take the bottle. Every time I give it to him, he spits it out and bellows."

"Perhaps you made it too hot," she said.

"Hot?"

"When you heated it."

He stared at the film of condensation on the glass. "It's cold," he said.

She looked at him as if she thought that if he had another brain, it would be lonely.

Stepping forward, she took the bottle from him. It was as close as she'd come to touching him since she'd tolerated having him usher her from the reception to the limo. ''Well, no wonder he's unhappy!''

''But it said on the note that I should keep the formula refrigerated!''

''Oh?'' She removed the nipple, put the open bottle in the microwave oven and set the timer to forty seconds. ''That was the extent of Marian's advice, was it? It never occurred to her that a complete set of instructions might be necessary?''

He didn't want to talk about Marian. He wanted to talk about *them;* about Julia and him, and how they were going to get their relationship back on the rails. It wasn't the most romantic moment, what with the baby screaming and all, but he tried anyway. ''You look beautiful, Julia. Like an angel.''

The microwave oven timer pinged. ''Here,'' she said, thrusting the bottle at him. ''Try it now.''

Okay, so his timing stank. He'd try another approach. "I'm not very good at this and you seem to know what you're doing." He hefted the baby in her direction. "Do you want to feed him?"

She froze, right down to her eyelashes. Absolutely nothing about her moved, and he knew he'd put his foot in it again.

"Sorry," he said, cringing inside at how mealymouthed he sounded. "I guess I'm pushing my luck."

"Yes," she said tightly. "I guess you can say, without fear of contradiction, that you are."

The baby latched on to the bottle tip as if he hadn't been fed in a week. For a few seconds, the only sound was the glug of the milk going down, and the kid's occasional grunting squeak of satisfaction.

Ben settled his hips against the kitchen counter and eyed his wife. "You're upset, I know. Anyone can see that and only a fool would deny you have the right. But you've got to know I didn't plan things to turn out this way. Hurting you is the last thing I ever wanted.''

''It would seem that Marian was the last thing you ever wanted,'' she said.

He swore. ''That's exactly the kind of remark that doesn't help, Julia. In fact, it's the kind of cheap shot I'd expect from your mother, not you.''

''Well, they do say, don't they, that if a man wants to know what kind of woman he's marrying, he only has to look at her mother? So if you're disappointed with what you ended up with, you can at least take comfort that you haven't come into the deal entirely empty-handed. *You* have a baby—which is a damned sight more than I've got.''

''You've got me,'' he said, curbing his irritation. They were both exhausted, physically and mentally, and he should never have started the conversation in the first place. ''You'll always have me.''

''I'm not sure I want you,'' she said.

''Julia…!''

But she'd gone, her bare feet whispering over the oak floor as lightly as thistledown in a breeze.

As though he didn't like not being the center of everyone's attention, the baby chose that moment to throw up.

"Holy...!" Ben rolled his eyes in despair and swabbed at his chest with a paper towel. "I don't know who it was who first said that good things come in little packages, Squirt, but he'd obviously never met you."

CHAPTER FOUR

SHE awoke the next morning to the splash of a fountain below her window and sunlit water reflections bouncing across the coffered ceiling. Just briefly, she wondered where she was, why she was alone, why there were no sheets on the bed and she was covered only by her peignoir.

Too quickly, the answers came to her as she recalled with stunning clarity the events of the previous day. The confrontation with Ben, his confession, her parents' barely concealed glee that he'd lived down to all their low expectations of him, not to mention the open curiosity of the wedding guests and their whispered speculation…oh, the indignity and pain of it all were beyond bearing!

Pushing her hair out of her face, she sat up in the middle of the mattress and looked around, searching for evidence to dispute the memories and prove them nothing more than a particularly bad dream. But the sight of her wedding dress lying where she'd tossed it in a heap on the floor, as neglected and forlorn as her marriage, gave proof positive that yesterday had been all too real.

The image of Marian Dawes had haunted her. Tiny, helpless, her big blue eyes swimming with pitiful tears, she was the kind of woman whose delicacy made fools of men; made them feel mighty and powerful and protective.

Maybe that had been her big mistake, Julia had thought, pacing the floor as the hours ticked by. When Ben said he wanted to wait until they were married before they made love, and then wait another couple of years to start the family she wanted so badly, maybe she should have pouted and broken down in tears. Appealed to his virility—because heaven knew, he had it in spades, and if she'd ever doubted it, the proof lay sleeping in the room at the other end of the house.

Dawn had been breaking behind Mount Baker before she'd fallen asleep finally but from the angle of the sun now, she guessed it must be about eight o'clock. The rest of the house was too quiet, the way a place is when no one else is home. Ben must have gone out for breakfast, or else to buy supplies for the baby.

Or else he'd left for good.

Refusing to acknowledge the momentary panic that thought gave rise to, Julia focused on more immediate concerns, such as finding something other to wear before she ventured from the room than a semitransparent nightdress or a crumpled wedding gown.

She needed a shower, fresh clothes and coffee strong and black, in that order. Only then could she face up to whatever the rest of the day—and her life—held in store.

She found her remaining luggage stacked outside her door, further indication that Ben had been up and about while she still slept. Dragging it into the room, she unpacked lingerie, a cotton sundress and sandals. There were towels in the ensuite bathroom, and shampoo, and plenty of hot water, testimony to the fact that not everything fell apart in the face of personal upheaval.

But there was no sign of Ben or the baby when she went downstairs, and no sign of coffee. Hardly surprising, since they hadn't expected to be taking up residence in the house for another month, so stocking up on groceries hadn't been at the top of their pre-wedding list of things to do.

No matter. She'd follow his example and go out for breakfast. There were coffee shops to spare along the beachfront.

But she got no further than the front door before coming face-to-face with her missing husband. And the child. Even though she'd known they were now a package deal, seeing them together came as a fresh shock of dismay. Would she ever get used to it, or was this sudden painful snag in her heart the way it was going to be for the rest of their lives?

"Hey," Ben said, fishing a bunch of pink rosebuds spattered with baby's breath from a pocket in the back of the infant seat, and offering it to her, ''where are you off to at this hour of the morning? It's not eight-thirty yet. These are from us, by the way.''

Us. The word that up until yesterday had cocooned her in the false security of believing that she and Ben had forged a magical, indestructible bubble of happiness that nothing and no one could puncture, took on an ominously darker complexion. There was room for only two in there and, suddenly, she was on the outside looking in. It was all she could do not to grab him by the throat and scream, ''The only *us* should be you and I. *Three* don't belong on a honeymoon!''

Of course, she did no such thing. Instead, she called on the pride that had carried her through yesterday's farce of a wedding celebration and, ignoring the roses, said, ''I thought it was much later. I thought I'd go out for breakfast.''

''No need. I've been shopping already.'' With his knee, he nudged at the four supermarket bags lined up on the step. ''I figured

I'd better stock up on stuff for the squirt here, so I bought for us while I was at it. We've got enough food to see us through a couple of meals at least.''

''Thank you anyway,'' she said, looking anywhere but at the baby strapped snugly in its car seat. ''I prefer to go out.''

''Prefer to be anywhere but with me, you mean.'' The edge in Ben's tone brought her gaze swinging back to his face. ''Why don't you just spit out the truth, Julia, instead of choking on it?''

''This has nothing to do with you and everything to do with the fact that I've had nothing to eat or drink since early last evening, and precious little in the twelve hours before that. Other events,'' she said pointedly, ''took precedence and for some strange reason, robbed me of my appetite.''

''Well, I can't fix everything that's gone wrong, but at least I can remedy that.'' He thrust the smallest of the bags at her. ''There's hot coffee, croissants and fruit salad in here. Take them outside and we'll eat on the kitchen patio. It's going to be another scorcher today, but I turned on the fountain this morning and put up the sun umbrella, so it should be reasonably pleasant out there.''

His attempts to normalize a situation that was anything but normal brought out a side of her nature as new and unwelcome to her as it undoubtedly was to him: stubborn, unreasonable, vindictive—they were words to leave her blushing inside. Sadly, they weren't enough to keep her from asking waspishly, ''Are you giving me orders now, Ben?''

''No. I'm trying like the devil not to alienate you any more than I already have. Why else would I be out buying you flowers and getting up at the crack of dawn to set the stage for a romantic breakfast for two?''

For two? Oh, that was a laugh! ''Do you seriously believe a few flowers and a fountain are all it's going to take to put things right between us?'' she said scornfully.

''No,'' he replied. ''But it seemed as good a place as any to start. You think I don't know I've screwed up? You think I can't see what

I've done to you—to us? I want to put things right, but I can't do it on my own. Whether you like it or not, you and I both are going to have to sit down and discuss things rationally to decide where, if anywhere, this marriage of ours is headed.''

''I thought we were headed for the kind of normal, happy life most couples expect once they've tied the knot. But so far, nothing about our marriage fits the norm, does it?''

''No. I hardly expected I'd become a father before I found out what it would be like to be a husband. Even less did I expect I'd be marrying someone other than the mother of my child.''

Every nasty, bruising thought she'd entertained in the last twelve hours supplanted common sense yet again. ''Is that your oblique way of telling me you think you married the wrong woman?''

He rolled his eyes and bundled the grocery supplies into his arms. ''Don't be childish, Julia. It doesn't suit you.''

Anger, guilt, disappointment and just plain, soul-destroying misery joined forces in a tide that swept the tattered shreds of her composure into oblivion. "How *dare* you criticize me?" she flared. "I'm the injured party here, not you. *None* of this mess is my fault!"

"I know," he said, and she flinched a little at the weariness in his voice. He'd always struck her as a tower of strength, godlike in his beauty and able to move mountains if he had to. It had never occurred to her that he might have feet of clay just like everyone else.

Remorse and a shadow of sympathy prompted her to reach for the grocery bags. "Give those to me. I'll take them to the kitchen."

"They're heavy. Take the baby instead."

"I'm stronger than I look." Without giving him the chance to raise further objections, she practically snatched the bags away from him and, hounded by a fresh wave of guilt, raced down the hall toward the back of the house.

What was wrong with her that she couldn't bring herself to look at the baby, let alone touch him? She might see herself as the most injured party in all this mess, but he was the most vulnerable. And the most blameless.

Miserably, she glanced around the custom-designed kitchen Ben had had built for her. An array of white lacquered cabinets, some with arched glass doors and lighted interiors to showcase the fine china and crystal wedding gifts she'd received; dark green granite counters and pale maple floors; the very latest and best in the way of appliances: it was a dream kitchen few women were lucky enough to own.

"I can't afford a live-in housekeeper," he'd told her when they'd first bought the house. "But if you'd like to have someone come in to do the cooking—?"

"No!" she'd exclaimed. "I'm not my mother, who couldn't find a can of soup in her house if her life depended on it. This is going to be *my* kitchen and I won't have some other woman making it hers."

She'd envisioned creating gourmet seven-course meals here when they entertained, having him perch on a stool and sip a glass of wine while she put the finishing touches to a quiet dinner for just the two of them. And she'd imagined how it would be when they eventually had children and they came home from school and sat at the breakfast bar enjoying milk and cookies she'd baked herself that morning.

But she'd never once thought that the first sack of disposable diapers and carton of powdered formula her husband bought would be for a baby that was his but not hers.

She heard footsteps approaching and pretended to be busy loading things in the refrigerator when Ben came up behind her. She felt his breath on her hair, and braced herself for the kiss she instinctively knew would follow.

His mouth fluttered against the side of her neck, warm and erotic. ''Leave that for now and come outside,'' he murmured in her ear, sliding his arm around her waist and cupping his hand under the slope of her breast. ''The coffee's getting cold.''

But he was hot. Hot and ready. The thrust of his hips against her bottom gave proof of exactly where he was coming from!

Furious as much with herself for the quivering response of her own flesh as she was with him for supposing he could seduce her so blatantly, she poked her head further inside the refrigerator. It didn't do much for his state of arousal, but it helped cool her down.

''Can't you see I'm busy?'' she said starchily, swatting him away. ''I don't want stuff going bad in this heat.''

He removed himself at once, leaving her with such an aching sense of loss that she could have wept. ''What stuff?'' he said, and there was that edge of impatience in his voice again. ''All I bought were a couple of steaks, some salad and a few dairy items, for Pete's sake! Hardly enough to make a morning's work out of. Or are you planning to climb in next to them when you're done, rather than face me?''

Straightening, she slammed the refrigerator closed. ''Fine! I'll sit outside. I'll drink the coffee. I'll eat a croissant. Will that make you happy?''

''No,'' he said shortly, flinging plastic knives and spoons on a tray next to the coffee and pastries. ''I suspect it's going to take a lot more than that to make either of us happy again. But this much I do know—until we arrive at some sort of resolution over what's happened, neither of us will be able to move forward. We're at an impasse here, Julia. Even you can't deny that. Where we go next and whether or not we both take the same path is what we've got to determine.''

''And what if I'm not ready to face that decision just yet?''

''That's what I'm most afraid of—your bottling everything up inside to the point that we never find our way back to each other again. We need to deal with this together, not apart.'' He held out his hand. ''Come on, Julia. Don't make me beg. The baby's upstairs and should sleep for a couple of hours. We won't be distracted by anything. Let's at least try to sort things out.''

Swinging away, she marched to the wrought-iron table and chairs on the patio outside the kitchen door. ''What's to sort out? You've already made up your mind what you're going to do and nothing I might have to say on the matter seems likely to change it.''

''I thought you'd made up your mind, too.'' He pinned her in a level gaze. ''You were given the option yesterday. You could have walked away from me and our marriage, but you chose not to. Call me thick if you like, but I took that to mean you were willing to give us a chance.''

''I wasn't prepared to make a snap decision, that's all. I wanted time to think things over.''

''And?''

She glared at him. ''And what?''

''I heard you pacing the floor all night. A reasonable man would assume you weren't doing it for the exercise. A reasonable man would assume it was because you couldn't sleep. A reasonable man would assume that was because you'd had a load of trouble dumped in your lap and you were trying to figure out a way to handle it.'' His mouth tightened formidably. ''I'm trying to be a reasonable man, Julia,'' he said, ''but you're coming dangerously close to pushing me beyond my limits. So instead of flinging my question back at me, try answering it. What conclusions did you arrive at during your long, sleepless night?''

''I didn't! You might have folded in the face of your former lover's pressure, but I won't be rushed on this, Ben, and that's final. Whatever I decide, it's going to take time. And a *reasonable* man wouldn't need to have me spell that out for him. He'd understand and back off, particularly in light of the embarrassment he's already put me through in front of my family and friends. How I'm ever going to face them all again I don't know! But I can tell you this—if you think your becoming a father is enough to give rise to a great uprush of maternal feelings in me, you're sadly mistaken.''

He tilted his chair backward, folded his arms over his chest and stretched out his long tanned legs. He was wearing denim cutoffs and a short-sleeved white cotton shirt and sneakers. He looked self-assured and invincible—and so sexy it was small wonder Marian Dawes had deserted her husband for him.

''There's more at stake here than your stiff-necked pride,'' he informed her. ''In case you haven't noticed, a child's future's hanging in the balance. I love you, make no mistake about that. But I won't tolerate your taking out your frustrations on that baby. If you decide I'm asking for more than you're prepared to give, you'll move on with your life and eventually find some other man to take my place. But that boy has already been abandoned by his mother. I'll see you in hell before I let you rob him of his father, too.''

She'd always known he had in him a steely strength that went beyond mere muscle power but this—the way he spoke to her, the harsh, uncompromising tone he adopted—*this* was a side of him she'd never seen before. Determined not to show how it rattled her, she said, ''You don't even know for sure that he *is* yours.''

"I know for sure that Wayne Dawes isn't his father. I know for sure that his date of birth makes it highly likely that I'm the only other candidate for the job."

"How can you know that?" she cried, slopping coffee all over the table in her agitation. "What makes you so sure you were the only one she was romping around in bed with? If you're telling the truth, you didn't even know Marian Dawes was married when you had your little affair with her."

The front legs of his chair slammed against the paved stones of the patio as he brought it upright again. Leaning across the table, he said, "There's no 'if' about it, Julia. I've never lied to you and I'm not about to start now. But if you're in any doubt about that, perhaps you should have dumped me before the ink dried on our marriage certificate. Because I won't live with a wife who doesn't believe I'm telling her the truth."

"How is it that I'm suddenly the villain of the piece?" she cried, too angry to care that he saw the tears filling her eyes.

He wiped one palm over his face and took a sip of his coffee. "There aren't any villains here, Julia, that's the whole point. There are only victims, and I'm sorry that you're one of them. I want to make things right again between us, but I can't do it by myself. You've got to want it, too. Last night..." He made a helpless gesture with his hand. "Shutting yourself in that bedroom, refusing even to listen to me, let alone have me touch you—sweetheart, that's not how two people in love mend what's broken between them."

She'd almost begun to soften toward him, almost felt the first stirrings of sympathy, but for all his conciliatory tone, they fled at his last remark. "What would you have had me do? Climb into bed with you as if we were on our honeymoon and we were happy as peach pie together? Did you think I could have sex with you and not find my mind filled with images of you doing the same things to Marian Dawes that you were doing to me?"

He regarded her as if she'd said something unspeakably obscene. "I did have sex with

Marian,'' he said flatly. ''But it never occurred to me that I'd have sex with you. I'd anticipated you and I would make love. To my mind, there's quite a difference between the two.''

''Well, you'll have to forgive me for not being quite as discerning. I haven't had your vast experience. I foolishly believed sleeping around was cheap, not to mention risky, so I saved myself for the man I married.''

Very deliberately, he put down his coffee container and stood up. ''Excuse me,'' he said. ''I hear the baby crying, and I'm concerned. He doesn't seem able to keep his food down and he's got a very suspicious bruise on his arm. I'm sure you'll enjoy not having me around while you finish your breakfast.''

She'd gone too far and she didn't need his carefully blank expression to realize it. But did she retrench before the damage grew worse? The old Julia would have; she'd have found it in herself to show a little remorse and compassion. But that person had died somewhere between cutting the wedding cake and leaving the reception in a hail of confetti. And the new Julia had such a core of bitterness to her that all she wanted to do was lash out at the person who'd brought her dreams crashing down about her ears, even if doing so hurt her as much as it hurt him.

She didn't like her replacement, but nor did she know how to get rid of her. She didn't even know how to shut her up. ''How convenient!'' her inner devil sneered. ''Is this how you're going to handle things in the future, Ben? By using Marian Dawes's baby as an excuse to avoid facing up to the fact that you've ruined the life we had planned?''

''I don't need an excuse. He's my baby, too, and until he's old enough to look out for himself, I'll put his interests above my own.''

''Even if it means losing me?''

He regarded her steadily, a long, penetrating gaze that had her fidgeting with fear inside. *Back off now or you'll live to regret it!* her common sense warned. But pride's more strident urging had her glaring back at him mutinously.

"I hope it won't come to that, Julia," Ben said evenly, "but if that's the choice you force me to make, then yes. Even if it means losing you."

Devastated by such uncompromising honesty, she cried, "I should have listened to my parents!"

"Perhaps you should have."

"They were right when they said I didn't know you well enough to marry you."

He shrugged and moved toward the patio door. "You already spelled that out to me yesterday. I don't care to go over the same tired ground again now, not with a month-old baby upstairs screaming for attention."

It was their first fight—well, first if she discounted the blowup at their wedding—and the way his nostrils flared in distaste as he brushed past her almost destroyed her. He'd never looked at her in such a way before, as if she were something nasty he'd found stuck to the underside of his shoe.

Of course, she'd said mean-spirited, disgusting things and she hated herself for it, so it didn't really surprise her that he'd responded so coldly. But for him actually to come out and admit that he'd choose the baby over her wounded her deeply. The little shows of tenderness between two people who've had a spat but who really love each other—a softly uttered apology, a touch, a kiss—they weren't going to fix what was broken this time. What divided them was too big, too permanent, too life-altering.

And she was making everything worse, letting pride and hurt feelings back her more tightly into a corner until she wondered if she'd ever find her way out again.

Instead of following him upstairs, as any woman with a shred of compassion in her soul would have done, she remained where she was, staring out at the brilliant blue sea until her eyes stung from the glare. And the distance between her and the man she loved, which had started with Marian Dawes's startling revelation the day before, yawned wider with each passing day until, instead of behaving like honeymooners so besotted with each other that they couldn't see straight, Julia and Ben were like strangers living under the same roof. Aloof, unsmiling, uncommunicative and so scrupulously polite that it made her teeth ache.

On the Tuesday, he came to where she was folding clothes in the laundry room. ''I'm driving into town,'' he said. ''Is there anything I can pick up for you while I'm out?''

''No,'' she said, unable to meet his glance for the pain she knew she'd see there. ''I can take care of whatever I might need.''

''Suit yourself,'' he said, and left. He didn't return until after lunch.

Later that same afternoon, a delivery truck drew up in the driveway and two men carried in a variety of baby furniture. Under his direction, they took it up to the room she and Ben had set aside as a future nursery.

''I never thought, when we bought this house, that someone else's baby would be sleeping in here,'' she remarked bitterly, when she saw.

"So where would you have me put him?" Ben said, in the politely indifferent tone that he'd perfected over the last few days. "In a closet? At the other end of the house where I can't hear him when he wakes up in the night? Or would you prefer that I buy a dog kennel and keep him at the bottom of the garden?"

"That's not fair!" she cried. "Stop painting me as the wicked stepmother in all this!"

He shrugged. "Why not? You're giving a pretty fair imitation of one."

"Perhaps if you'd taken the trouble to discuss the matter with me before you—"

"*Discuss?* Don't make me laugh, Julia! I'm tired of begging you to talk to me. You can hardly stand to breathe the same air as I do, let alone engage in rational conversation."

"Well, I'm engaging you now," she replied, stung. "You shouldn't be putting the crib so close to the window. If there was an earthquake, the glass could shatter all over *your son.*"

He paused in the middle of lowering the mattress into place. "Where do you suggest I put it, then?"

"It's not my decision to make," she said, perversely retreating into the hard shell of reserve that had become so much a part of her in recent days. "I was just pointing out something I thought everyone knew."

He skewed a glance her way and rubbed his chin thoughtfully. "I don't know beans about looking after a baby. I could use some help."

Oblique though it was, she recognized his comment as an invitation for her to become involved with his child. But even as a small part of her warmed to the offer, another, much larger part resented it. This was *their* house, *their* nursery, and it should have been *their* baby sleeping in the gleaming new crib with rabbits painted on the headboard.

"Then you ought to have picked up a couple of child care books while you were out on your shopping spree," she muttered.

His mouth twisted. "There are a lot of things I ought to have done, Julia, including, I'm beginning to think, waiting a bit longer to ask you to marry me. If I'd shown a little restraint in that respect, I might have spared us both a lot of painful regrets.''

The hurt he inflicted with that remark left her so breathless that she turned and literally fled, not just from the room, but from the house, too. Grabbing her purse and keys, she raced out to her car and drove away with no fixed plan in mind beyond knowing that she needed to pour out her heart to someone who cared enough about her to be objective.

Of course, she couldn't go home to her parents. They couldn't be objective about anything to do with Ben if their lives had depended on it. But there was someone she could turn to and almost as if it knew exactly where she was headed, the car nosed its way through the summer tourist traffic to the freeway running north to Vancouver.

CHAPTER FIVE

"I LET him chase me out of my own house, Amma," Julia wailed an hour later, sobbing out her story to Felicity and dripping tears all over her grandmother's silk-cushioned French sofa.

"Nonsense," Felicity said, plopping a box of tissues in Julia's lap. "You let that poor benighted Marian Dawes chase you away. I'm surprised at you, Julia. I thought you were made of sterner stuff."

Indignation put a dent in Julia's woebegone histrionics. "As if I care about her!" she whimpered.

"That's sheer foolishness, Julia! Of course you care about her. This whole *business* is about her. Or are you trying to tell me you'd be reacting the same way if Ben had no connection to that baby beyond having found him

106

abandoned on the side of the road and bringing him home for you to care for?''

Leaving Julia to ponder the truth of that question, Felicity went to the rosewood cabinet where she kept her liquor and poured two glasses of sherry. ''It's time to stop feeling sorry for yourself and start facing reality, my angel, so dry those useless tears and take a healthy swig of this,'' she said, returning and placing one of the glasses in Julia's hand. ''I have great faith in the restorative powers of good sherry.''

Half a glass later, Julia admitted, ''You're right on all counts, of course. It is about Marian. I'm so angry with her for her timing and for how she's behaved.''

''You're angry with Ben, too, Julia. Let's be brutally honest here.''

''Yes, I am. And I'm disappointed in him, too.'' She looked anywhere but at her grand-mother. ''And I guess I'm retaliating by refusing to acknowledge the baby.''

''Yes,'' Felicity said briskly. ''Well, keep it up and you'll lose your husband. He gave you the chance to walk away and you chose not to, but if this is how you intend to treat him, you'd have done him a bigger favor by leaving him at the outset. Because the way you're going about things, you're likely to find yourself free of him and all the baggage he's brought with him into this marriage, whether you want to or not.''

She took a sip of her sherry, then went on, ''And I'll tell you this. He's the kind of man women find attractive. He has a great deal to offer. If you're not interested in the job of being his wife, it won't be too long before someone else offers to step into your shoes. Is that you want? Have you fallen out of love as quickly as you fell in?''

Julia stared at the veil of liquid draping the inner rim of her glass. ''I don't know anymore, and that's the truth. I've asked myself a hundred times, if all this had come to light before we were married, would I have called off the wedding? Or has it more to do with the fact that Ben had what was obviously a hot and heavy affair with a married woman that ended only months before he met me? Or is it that there's someone else demanding all the attention I was used to having him give to me?'' She lifted her shoulders helplessly. ''I'm too confused to sort out the answers.''

For a few minutes, Felicity didn't reply. She seemed to be debating the kindest way to deliver her next chunk of grandmotherly wisdom. She patted a cushion into place, played with her pearls and swung a delicate ankle.

''Ben has let you down, there's no question of that, Julia,'' she finally said, ''and I imagine he'd be willing to kiss your toes daily for the next sixty years, if that's what it would take to make you forgive him. But you're not the only one with pride and when a man's is trampled in the dust, he can become very intractable, as you're likely to find out if you keep on punishing him.''

''If you're suggesting I should—!''

Felicity shook her head. ''I'm suggesting nothing. Only you know how far you're willing to go to keep your marriage intact. All I'm saying is, you'd do well to figure it out before it's too late. Because if Ben gets to the end of his rope with the way things are and walks out, I doubt you'll ever persuade him to come back again. He's had too much experience of not being wanted, as you very well know, to tolerate a wife's rejection kindly.''

''That might be all you're saying, Amma, but what you're thinking is that I should go home and just forget everything that's happened.''

''Wrong again, my darling. The only way I'd advise you to do that is if I was convinced that you're ready to accept the decision he's made regarding his son. But I don't think you are. I think you're willfully closing your mind and heart to that little boy, and I'm rather ashamed of you.''

''What if he's not Ben's son?'' Julia blurted, stunned that the grandmother who'd encouraged her throughout every phase of her life could take such a hard line now, when she most needed her support.

''Why can't you see that genetics are no longer important? What matters is that that little boy desperately needs people willing to step into the role of parents and give him the kind of loving home he deserves. That Ben is prepared to do that, without benefit of official proof that he's the natural father, doesn't lessen his worth, it adds to it. As for poor misguided Marian Dawes, maybe she slept with fifteen different lovers and doesn't know which one is the father, but at least when she decided to give away her child, she made sure she chose a man with the backbone and integrity to take on the job.''

''Are you defending her?'' Julia was outraged.

''It's not my place to defend or condemn. But I'll say this. There aren't many women brave enough to admit that they're not cut out for motherhood and I applaud her for at least having the courage to recognize her own unsuitability for the part. I'm sure the decision has, and will, cost her dearly. But I'm equally certain that that baby shouldn't also be made to pay the price.''

"And you think that's what I'm doing—punishing him?"

"Yes. Because you *are* the maternal type. You've always wanted children. You just don't want this particular little soul. And I'm very much afraid that he's part of the marriage equation now. So if remaining Mrs. Ben Carreras is at all important to you, you're going to have to come to terms with that."

Julia almost gagged on her sherry. "I'm not up to glossing over everything and smiling till my face aches, just to save my marriage!"

"I'm not suggesting you should."

"It seems to me that you are. You think that if I don't want to lose my husband, I ought go home, fling myself into his arms and pretend I've had some sort of epiphany about the baby and can't wait to take on two a.m. feedings."

"Oh, get over yourself, Julia!" Felicity snorted with indignation, a rare occurrence with her but not without precedent. The difference was, she usually directed such outbursts at her daughter-in-law, not her granddaughter. "You don't have the right to try to hang on to Ben unless you're willing to accept his baby, too, but you have even less right to try to bamboozle him! Merely going through the motions of motherhood isn't good enough. Not only does the baby deserve better, so does Ben. Furthermore, he's no fool. He'd see through that sort of act in a flash. For heaven's sake, child, put aside your silly pride and focus instead on the thing that really matters— namely the love you and Ben have for one another. That's what's going to see you through this unhappy time.''

Julia slumped against the cushions. ''I'm sorry if this disappoints you, Amma, but I'm not ready to make such a leap of faith quite yet.'' With her forefinger, she traced the outline of a damask rose on the arm of the sofa. ''Perhaps I need to put a little distance between me and the situation before I can sort out my true feelings.''

''Well, darling,'' Felicity sighed, ''when all's said and done, you're the only one who can decide what's best for you. But please try to remember why you fell in love with Ben in

the first place and don't be in too much of a
hurry to give up on him. At the risk of sounding trite, let me remind you of that old saying
not to throw out the baby with the bathwater.
If you're half the person I've always believed
you to be, you'll keep that in mind, both literally and figuratively, as you work through
your decision.''

When he first heard Julia's car roar off down
the driveway, Ben blamed himself. He'd been
insensitive—hell, he didn't seem able to be
anything *but* these days! Already, she thought
all he was really interested in was getting her
in the sack. Given that he wound up with an
erection every time he got within six feet of
her, he could hardly blame her.

And if his being permanently horny wasn't
enough to tick her off, he was also short-
tempered, worried, exhausted and feeling profoundly sorry for himself. Not exactly a barrel
of laughs to be around.

As for the business of the nursery…!

More tired than he'd ever been in his life before, he sank down on the edge of the unmade bed in the master suite and buried his face in his hands. Sheesh! Even a moron would know better than to lay claim to the one room in the house originally intended to be set up as the nursery for children not yet conceived, let alone born!

Trouble was, he *wasn't* much more than a walking moron these days. The baby never seemed to sleep for more than an hour at a stretch, and whatever technique there was to getting a kid that age to burp after every meal was beyond anything Ben had been able to figure out.

How else to account for the almost constant vomiting? Then there were the bruises, fading now but still visible and too closely matching the marks left by a man's rough hand for Ben's peace of mind.

I have to make sure he's safe, Marian had said, and he was afraid he knew now why ''safe'' had been the word she used.

Heaving a sigh, he lay back on the bed with his legs hanging over the side and his arms folded behind his head, and stared at the ceiling. For once, the house was so blessedly quiet he could actually hear the faint swish of waves breaking on the beach below the garden.

The next thing he knew, there were long shadows fingering their way across the room and the baby monitor on the bedside table was emitting little outraged squawks from the nursery.

Bleary-eyed and groggy, Ben hauled himself to a sitting position and checked the time. Six o'clock? Hell, the squirt had slept nearly three hours! As for Julia, she'd been gone almost four.

The realization lodged in his stomach like a great soggy lump of week-old bread. Where the devil was she? Had she come back while he slept, or had she left for good?

Rolling his shoulders to work out the kinks from where he'd been sleeping, he staggered to the window and looked out. There was no sign of her car but the door to the garage where she usually kept it was closed, so it could be that he'd simply not heard her come home.

The baby was burbling to himself, funny little snotty noises, but at least he wasn't crying. Turning from the window, Ben decided he had enough time to go downstairs and, while a bottle of formula was warming in the microwave oven, check the garage to see if Julia's car was there.

It wasn't. Nor was there a message on the telephone answering machine, or a note on the kitchen counter to indicate that she'd come back and gone out again. And if that wasn't enough to sour his mood even further, he accidentally set the oven timer for four minutes instead of forty seconds, and nuked the formula to boiling point.

And the baby was screaming. Again.

The baby! Still feeling as if he'd been hit across the side of the head with a two-by-four, Ben directed a breath out of the corner of his mouth and took another bottle of formula out of the refrigerator.

He shoved it in the oven, made sure he'd set the timer properly this time and paced to the window overlooking the garages. Still no sign of Julia, but the baby was certainly making his presence felt. Whatever else he might be lacking, the kid had a great set of lungs!

Sooner or later, he was going to have to come up with another name for the boy, he thought, gnawing on a hangnail and continuing to scan the driveway anxiously. He couldn't go on calling him Kid or Squirt forever and he wasn't interested in Junior, which had been Marian's inspired choice—presumably in the hope that he'd turn out to be her husband's offspring.

His original idea—to hold off making a decision in the hope that Julia would come around and they'd choose something together—didn't seem likely to happen, given the present rate of nonprogress in their relationship. They were drifting further apart with every passing day.

Up in the nursery, the baby increased the decibel screech level another notch. Amazing how much noise such a pint-size body could produce!

''Hold your fire, Squirt,'' Ben muttered and, grabbing the formula, took the stairs two at a time, screwing the cap on the bottle as he went and splashing a dollop of milk on his arm to make sure it wasn't too hot.

The baby had managed to twist himself around so that his head was jammed up against the side of the crib. He'd thrown up, as well— mostly in his ear, which surely took extraordinary talent. As for the diaper, it had more or less exploded!

''Holy sh—ipmates!'' Shuddering, Ben tackled the rear end first, no mean feat given that the kid was pitching a major fit at being left to starve for so long. ''Keep still, you little toad, or we'll both need to take a bath!''

By the time he'd got that end under control and stuffed the formula in the other end, another hour had slipped by, still with no sign of Julia. Propping the snoozing baby against his shoulder, he went through the burping routine with his usual lack of success, pacing the floor the whole time and keeping an ear open for the sound of a car pulling up in the driveway.

Just before seven-thirty, the phone rang and startled the baby into letting loose with a mighty belch and spitting up all over Ben's neck. "Sorry if I caught you at a bad moment, dear," Felicity Montgomery said, when he explained why he was sounding just a bit harried, "but with a new baby in the house, there's really never a good time to call. I won't keep you, though. I just wanted to have a quick word with Julia."

"Me, too," Ben said, choosing his words with care. He liked Felicity and he rather thought she wouldn't take sides if she knew the mess his marriage was in, but he saw no reason to broadcast that he hadn't the foggiest idea where his wife was. Blood was thicker than water, after all, and the last thing he needed was for his in-laws to get wind of the way things were. They'd be tap-dancing on the ceiling! "She went out this afternoon and isn't back yet."

The utter silence this item of news produced told him plenty, even before Felicity recovered enough to say, "That's odd. I thought she was going straight home when she left here."

"Oh," he said, trying like the blazes to sound unconcerned, "she mentioned doing some shopping downtown and probably got caught in commuter traffic."

At this hour, idiot? You won't fool anyone with that excuse, least of all a lady as sharp as Felicity!

"Well, there's no urgency," Felicity said. "It's just that I forgot to mention when she was here that all those wedding gifts people brought to the reception are stored in my garage and I wanted to find out when would be a good time to arrange for them to be delivered to your place. Get her to give me a call when she has a moment, Ben, and we'll set something up."

"I'll do that, Felicity. And thanks for calling."

"You're welcome, dear. Kiss that sweet baby for me."

"I will," he said, horrified to hear his voice cracking.

Steamed, he hung up. Felicity, who had no reason to give a hoot about him or anyone connected with him, could show a little kindness toward his baby, but his AWOL wife—the woman who'd promised before God and half the social elite of West Vancouver to love him for better or worse *and* who'd elected to stand by that promise—couldn't bring herself to remain in the same room with the kid.

Switching the baby to his other arm, Ben gingerly felt the soggy spot on his shirt collar. "That's the third time today you've left me smelling like week-old milk left out in the afternoon sun," he told the boy. "We're going to have to do something about your aim, kiddo!"

He'd bought a swing that morning, one of those contraptions that wound up and kept an infant content and safe while whoever was in charge took time for other essentials. Carting the whole works into the master bathroom, he strapped the baby in place and adjusted the speed of the motor. Fascinated by the motion and seeming perfectly content, the baby gazed around with big blue eyes and hiccuped.

"I'll make you a deal," Ben said, shucking off his clothes. "You stay happy while I grab a shower, then we'll hike back downstairs and you get to watch while I throw some sort of dinner together. We guys have to stick together, you know."

Except it shouldn't be like that. For all that things had been tough for his parents—and his father had screwed up more times than Ben cared to remember—his mom had stood by her man to the bitter end.

He'd thought he and Julia would be the same, yet here he was, alone in the house they'd bought together, with no idea if she was ever coming home again.

I'm rather ashamed of you. Ashamed... ashamed...ashamed...! Felicity's words hounded Julia as she drove south on Highway 99, repeating themselves over and over in her mind and leaving her feeling small and undeserving of the unconditional love her grand-mother had showered on her all her life. How was it that she couldn't show the same gen-erosity toward Ben? What flaw in her makeup had her holding back, and making an innocent baby pay the price?

She knew the answer. It wasn't that she couldn't love the little mite; it was that she was afraid to—not because he might not be Ben's real son, but because he most likely was.

A week ago, she'd have staked her life on the conviction that love could overcome any obstacle. Ben was her rock, her life, her future. Together they were indestructible, indivisible. The world was their oyster.

But in the space of half an hour, that belief had been rocked with an uncertainty that had continued to fester in the days since. From the moment Marian Dawes gate-crashed the wed-ding and made her dramatic revelation, all Julia's preconceived notions of happy-ever-after had flown out of the window.

She was so immersed in her thoughts that she missed the turnoff for Crescent Beach and had to drive several miles farther before she could leave the freeway and take the narrow road winding along the beach into White Rock.

The receding tide had left behind milk-warm pools in the vast stretch of pale beach—a treasure land of discovery for a little boy. When the baby was old enough...

When the baby was old enough, he might well be living with his birth mother again. And his father!

The realization brought her smack up against the true heart of the problem. It wasn't that she couldn't forgive Ben or that she couldn't love his son. It was fear of losing one or both that held her back, and she knew why.

She'd been nine when someone gave her a kitten, and for a few wonderful weeks, the loneliness that had been such a part of her childhood had been eased by the comfort of that warm, furry little body cuddled up close to her. It had waited for her to come home from school each day and slept on her bed each night.

But it had also scratched the furniture and broken a priceless Ming vase, and one day she came back to find it gone. "We got rid of it, of course," her mother had told her. "It didn't belong in a house like ours."

What if Marian decided her baby didn't belong in the Carreras household, and decided to take her child away again? *That* was the real crux of the matter. The difference lay in the fact that Julia was no longer a helpless child. She was an adult and big enough to fight for what she wanted.

Shortly before ten-thirty, she started the car and turned it toward home. The standoff between her and Ben had gone on long enough. It was time to start making their marriage work.

He must have paced to the front door a hundred times. And as the hours passed, what had begun as anxiety metamorphosed into gut-wrenching fear insulated with anger. When the beam of headlights finally arced across the window, followed by the familiar growl of her car inching its way into the garage, something inside him snapped and blind fury took hold of him.

She came in quietly, tiptoeing like a thief toward the stairs. He could see her quite clearly in the moon-dappled hall and waited until she was level with the open door to the library before he flicked on the lamp and showed himself seated at the desk.

Startled, she spun around. "I thought you'd be in bed," she exclaimed softly.

"I thought you might be dead," he said, tamping down with a marked lack of success the urge to roar at her like a demented lion. "I was so sure something had happened to you that I phoned the police and every hospital in the lower mainland."

"Oh, Ben, I'm sorry!"

She started toward him, her eyes wide pools of distress and her mouth soft and tender. Once, that would have been all it took for him to forget everything but that she was home safe and within arm's reach where she belonged. Now, it just wasn't enough. Too much had happened; too much resentment and mistrust had sprung up between them.

"The next time you decide to take off, Julia, do me the courtesy of telling me where you're going and how long you expect to be away." He paused a second or two, then added heavily, "Always assuming there *is* a next time, of course."

She stopped in her tracks and stared at him. "What do you mean, 'assuming there *is* a next time'? What are you trying to say?"

"That your little sulking spell's gone on long enough. I'm tired of it, Julia. In fact, I'm perilously close to being tired of you. I've got my hands full coping with one baby. I don't need another, especially not one who'll turn twenty-four in another couple of weeks. It's long past time for you to grow up, my dear."

Her smothered gasp hung in the air a moment, then she straightened her shoulders in that proud Montgomery way her mother had perfected to a fine art. "I see. And are you at all interested in knowing how I feel?"

Flinging the question in his face like that, as if, yet again, he'd committed some unspeakable sin by daring to spit out the truth, ignited him to further rage. Lunging to his feet, he strode around the desk and bore down on her. "As a matter of fact, no. For once, it's how I feel that counts. I don't like being treated like dirt. I don't like being left to cool my heels while the woman I married debates whether or not she's willing to behave like a wife. I don't like having to account to her for things that happened before I even met her. I've recited mea culpas without end and they've done me not one iota of good. To put it very bluntly, my dear, I've had it up to here with pussyfooting around your sensibilities."

For a second or two, she stood her ground and glared him down unflinchingly. "Are you threatening to exercise your conjugal rights, regardless of whether or not I agree?"

Was he? Heaven knew, his wanting her never let up. Deep, powerful, obsessive, it left him so hollow with need that he hardly knew how he kept his hands to himself.

His personal code of ethics had saved him from disgracing himself throughout the days since the wedding and it came to his rescue now. ''I'd rather be dead,'' he said stonily. ''To my way of thinking, there's a name for that kind of behavior that no man worth his salt would ever countenance. Wife or lover or one-night stand, if a woman doesn't come to a man willingly, he's guilty of rape. And wouldn't mother-in-law dearest love to hang *that* label around my neck! So, no, Julia. You can retire to your virginal bedchamber safe in the knowledge that I don't believe in droit de seigneur.''

He touched a nerve. Like a balloon leaking air, all the umbrage seeped out of her. Collapsing into one of the armchairs next to the fireplace, she buried her face in her hands. She wasn't crying. At least, he didn't think she was because she didn't make a sound and her shoulders weren't shaking. She just sat hunched over so that her hair fell forward and he couldn't read her expression.

When at last she spoke again, her voice was muffled. ''You're right, and I'm so ashamed. This is all my fault.''

If she'd railed at him some more, or tried to excuse her behavior, or even flatly denied his allegations, he could have met fire with fire. But he was no match for her complete surrender. Everything about her, from the sweet curve of her spine to the pale skin at the nape of her neck, seemed so…vulnerable. It left him feeling like some brutish hunter terrorizing a rare and beautiful creature too gentle to protect itself.

In the blink of an eye, all the outrage that had built such a fine head of justified steam during the hours of her absence turned to mush inside him and all he knew was an aching need to hold her, to stroke away her misery, to comfort her.

Touching her too soon, though, would merely complicate matters. Despite everything, he was still hungry for her, no question about that, and talking himself into satisfying the craving would take little persuasion, but it wouldn't resolve the wider issues separating them.

So he went back to his chair—on the other side of the desk and about as far away from her as he could get, short of leaving the room completely—and said, "Let's back up a bit before we make things worse. I'm sorry I yelled. I was worried when you were gone so long, and when you finally got home, I overreacted. Seems to me we've both been doing a lot of that lately."

She lifted her head, and he saw that she was crying after all, a silent, heartbreaking trickle of helpless tears. "I know," she said, wiping at her cheeks with the back of her hand. "I'm sorry. I should never have suggested you'd force yourself on me. I know you never would. In fact, I wouldn't blame you if you decided you hated me."

Her remorse was killing him. *Go to her now, you dolt, and let nature take its course!* his insidious libido urged. *It's the fastest route to reconciliation and nothing she's said or done justifies your putting her through this kind of hell.*

''I could never hate you, Julia,'' he said, wrestling with his inner devils, ''and this isn't about who's to blame. It's about you and me salvaging our marriage. It's cracking badly, and if we don't start effecting some sort of damage control, it's going to fall apart.''

''No!'' she cried, springing up from her chair. ''I don't want that, Ben, I honestly don't! You're the most important person in my life. You *are* my life! And I want us to be a family, I really do.''

''I'd like to believe that, honey,'' he said, ''but I can't help feeling you're speaking more out of fear and pride than conviction. It's not always easy admitting to the mistakes we make but we owe it to ourselves and each other to confront the facts. And the way I see it, if our staying married is going to be an uphill struggle for the next however many years, then I've got to tell you now, Julia, that I can't do it. I *won't* do it. I won't bring up a child in a house filled with discord and reproach just so that we can save face with other people.''

''I'm not asking you to,'' she cried, coming around the desk and reaching for him.

Another couple of steps and she'd be touching him. In anticipation of her soft hands sliding around his neck, of her sweet body pressing up against his, his flesh tightened, increasing the perpetual ache in his groin. He wanted her so badly, he could taste it.

''Stop right there,'' he said huskily, ''or I won't be responsible for what I do, and I've got to live with myself tomorrow. I just told you how I feel about my so-called husbandly right. Please don't make a liar out of me.''

''What if I don't want you to be responsible?'' she murmured. ''We've waited so long, Ben, and let so many other things come between us.''

''And we can wait a bit longer,'' he said, forcing the reply past the ravings of a mind gone mad with frustrated passion. ''I won't use sex as a means of trying to manipulate—''

''Not even if I'm begging you to?''

She was so close by then that her perfume filled his senses. He felt her fingers slide over his jaw and trace a path along his mouth. The impact shot the length of him like an arrow, with the usual incendiary result. Risking permanent injury, he attempted to cross his legs and maintain at least a modicum of dignity.

"Julia, please...!" The warning whistled past his lips as if he were in the throes of an asthma attack.

"Please just shut up and kiss me," she whispered, dipping her head so that her breath fanned his eyelashes. Cripes, even *they* were getting aroused! "I don't think I can go through another night without your arms around me."

And just in case he hadn't figured out exactly what she was really saying, she took his hand—which resisted her move with all the determination of a limp lettuce—and placed it on her breast. He felt the firm warmth of her flesh beneath her cotton dress, the surge of her nipple against his palm, and almost had a heart attack.

"No...!" His protest emerged on a strangled moan. "I don't want you giving in to impulse tonight, then regretting it in the morning."

"I promise you I won't. I've never been more clearheaded in my life." Sidling behind his chair, she cushioned his head against her breasts, swirled her tongue in his ear and let her fingers walk an erotic path all the way down his chest to his waist.

Doing his best to shake hands with her, the yardstick of his manhood outdid itself, rising to the occasion in grand style.

Julia's reaction almost moved Ben to tears. "Oh," she said, on a breath as frail as a petal, and then, with a curiosity at once artlessly curious and wickedly possessive, she touched him.

In his mind, he still wasn't sure making love was the right way to go about fixing everything that had gone wrong between them. But his mind wasn't in charge anymore. Julia was.

He knew when he was beaten. "Okay, you win," he said hoarsely and like a lamb being led to the slaughter, allowed her to pull him up out of the chair and steer him toward the stairs.

CHAPTER SIX

PIANO music played in the background, the cocktail lounge variety, soft and romantic. The bed, a carved antique affair that they'd chosen together on a shopping spree a month before the wedding, loomed in the middle of the room, its rumpled sheets awash with shadows like dusky snow on miniature mountains. *The marriage bed,* Ben had called it, the day they'd found it, and whispered outrageous promises in her ear that had left her blushing.

Julia wasn't blushing now, though. Suddenly unsure of her ability to carry off such an out-and-out seduction, she was frozen inside, a deep, penetrating chill that extended to her fingertips.

What was she supposed to do next? Undress him? Strip off her own clothes? Wait for him to make the next move?

His eyes glittered watchfully in the moon-light. ''It's okay if you're having second thoughts,'' he said.

She shook her head. ''I'm not.''

She meant to sound confident, but the quiver in her voice gave her away. A scared rabbit, that's what she was, afraid to face what lay ahead and afraid to turn away.

''Come here,'' Ben commanded softly, and pulled her into his arms.

He had not held her like that—tenderly, yearningly—in so long that she melted against him in relief. Perhaps not so very much had changed between them, after all.

His thigh nudged hers; his hand pressed against the small of her back. Without con-scious thought, she followed his lead, so pre-occupied with wondering what her next move should be that it took her a moment or two to realize they were dancing.

''It's been a long time since we did this,'' she whispered, the shaking that had played such havoc with her insides spreading to the rest of her.

"Not really," he said, grazing the wide scooped neckline of her dress with his mouth. "It just seems like forever. I've missed you, Julia."

"How can you miss someone you're at odds with?" A foolish question, as she knew from personal experience, given that she'd ached for him every minute that she'd been opposing him, but nervousness had her babbling like the proverbial brook. "I'd have thought you'd be glad to see the back of me."

With a muffled snort of laughter, he pushed her dress off her shoulders and down past her breasts. Loose and full, it fell around her ankles with a soft sigh, leaving her standing before him with nothing on but her underwear.

"Right now, I'm more interested in the front of you," he said.

She felt horribly naked and woefully inadequate. When she'd pictured the first time she and Ben made love, she'd imagined herself freshly bathed...perfumed...draped in chiffon against a background of flattering candlelight. Not wearing sandals and a plain white cotton bra and underpants. Not with her hair all tangled, and her skin smelling of the sea, and traces of tears smearing her face.

Instinctively, she crossed her arms over her breasts and tried to turn away from him, but he would have none of it. "I want to look at you," he said, pinning her hands in his.

Grateful for the shadowed light, she allowed him to scrutinize her and prayed he would not be disappointed at what he saw. She'd witnessed too much disillusionment in his eyes recently to endure seeing it again now. Whatever else had gone wrong between them over the past week, *this* moment had to remain unspoiled.

He was silent for the longest time; so long, in fact, that she grew flustered under his gaze. "I know I'm no great beauty, Ben," she said, because it was true. Her waist was fashionably narrow but her breasts were small and her legs, though long and slender enough, were unremarkable.

"You're a beauty to me," he said, his gaze scouring her from head to foot. "I find you lovely beyond anything I'd ever imagined."

He dipped his head and caught her in a kiss that stole over her lips as sweetly as the dawn. "I want to touch you," he murmured against her mouth then, guiding her hands inside his shirt and laying them against the solid planes of his chest, added, "I want you to touch me."

He felt warm, strong, vibrantly masculine— and more. Honorable, courageous and able and willing to protect those he loved. Eyes suddenly gushing tears, she stared at him. He is my husband, she thought wonderingly. He is my *husband!*

For the first time since their wedding day— perhaps the first time ever—the word had real meaning for her.

"Don't be afraid," he said, mistaking the reason for her tears. "We can take this as slowly as you like."

Mutely, she nodded, because even if she'd known how to answer him, she couldn't have spoken for the aching fullness in her throat.

He slid his hands past her waist and holding her by the hips, began to move, taking her with him in slow rhythm to the music still playing quietly in the background.

He guided her with gentle, insistent pressure, drawing her closer with every step and leaving her acutely conscious of how little separated them. Apart from his shirt, he was wearing only a pair of beachcombers made of lightweight material and held up by a drawstring.

She glanced down. All it would take was a tug....

"Do it," he said.

"What?" She looked up at him, too taken aback by his mind-reading ability to be embarrassed at being caught staring.

"Get rid of them, sweetheart, or I will."

A blush crept over her face, burning all the way up from her toes. "How did you know...?"

He inched her even closer until she was so tightly fused against him that not even a beam of light could have come between them. She felt the heat and vigor of him straining against the thin fabric of the slacks, the subtle thrust of him against her belly as he moved to the music.

"Male intuition," he said, tracing an intimate line over the curve of her bottom to the inside crease of her thigh.

A jolt of electricity, so swift and unexpected that it startled her, shot throughout her body to end with throbbing awareness low in her abdomen.

He'd touched her before, but never as intimately and never with such devastating results. She found herself pressing against him, aching and trembling; almost sobbing for a completion she barely comprehended.

But he understood. Releasing her, he pulled loose the drawstring at his waist, kicked off his pants and tore off his shirt, all with an economy of movement that would have impressed her far more if she hadn't found her attention riveted on the splendor of his near nudity.

In slow motion, her gaze rolled down his torso, taking in his width of shoulder and chest, his flat stomach and narrow waist, the symmetry and structure of his lean hips. And finally, because there was no ignoring it, that other part: the part she'd wondered and fantasized about so often in the months that had gone before; the part that would change her forever, taking away the virginity she'd preserved for this man she'd married, but giving back in return a sense of union and intimacy beyond anything she could begin to imagine.

His skin glowed dark caramel in contrast to his white briefs, which shone like a beacon in the dim light, spotlighting the powerful virility of him, which even she, inexperienced as she was, recognized as formidable. Bemused and quite of its own accord, her hand reached out and dared to touch.

Shocked by her own temerity, she sprang away from him as if she'd been burned. Maybe she even gasped aloud, because she heard laughter in his voice when he said, "What's the matter?"

"You're...*it's* so...big!" The observation, unsophisticated to the point of being childish to her ears, didn't seem to strike him the same way.

His grin rivaled his briefs in brilliance. ''Well, thanks, honey! I was hoping you'd be pleased.''

Pleased? She was terrified! How was it possible for a man and a woman to...?

Abruptly, the thought sheared away, too overwhelming to be entertained. Had this been what her mother was alluding to when, during one of the many attempts she'd made to dissuade Julia from the marriage, she'd warned, ''Sex isn't very dignified, you know. But it's a wife's duty to accommodate her husband, whether or not she's in the mood. Because he'll *always* be in the mood and that, my dear, is but one of the many crosses you'll have to bear.''

Perhaps Ben sensed her sudden doubt because, very gently, he took Julia's wrist and raising it to his mouth, sewed a seam of slow, moist kisses all the way up her inner arm. He pressed a kiss at the soft triangle of skin that connected to her shoulder, and another at her ear, her jaw, her eyelids and her nose. At last and with scrupulous dedication, he kissed her mouth, deeply.

And all the time that he was kissing her, he was touching, too, drawing his forefinger in a long, slow sweep from the hollow of her throat and straight down between her breasts to her midriff, then down even farther, to the one part of her he'd never touched before.

He left fire in his wake, a torching lava of sensation that bubbled wildly through her veins to converge between her thighs.

She swallowed and pressed her legs together, ashamed of the sudden flood of fierce heat dampening her underwear like tears too long suppressed. But her attempt at modesty misfired badly, trapping his hand in the very spot she most sought to shield.

Appalled, she tried to relax, another faulty move because, seizing the moment, his thumb immediately trespassed with stunning audacity inside the high-cut leg of her panties, and parted the slick folds of her flesh.

At his touch, an arrow of sensation arced through her, so sweetly painful, so pleasurably sinful, that it made a mockery of her former diffidence. "Ah…!" she whimpered on a long breath, opening for him and helpless to contain the shudders wracking her body.

With a low rumble of satisfaction, Ben caught her up in his arms and carried her to the bed. The sheets whispered against her bare skin, a small sibilant welcome as if to say, *It's about time you got here. We've been waiting all week for the honeymoon to start.*

Still battered by the passions he'd aroused in her, Julia barely knew how she and Ben came to be fully naked. Their clothing seemed to melt away in the driving need to press skin to skin. No longer timid or afraid, she set about discovering her husband, touching him everywhere and reveling in the knowledge that *she* was the reason his flesh surged against her, hot and urgent and completely beyond his ability to control.

Not that she had much say in how she responded to him! As her body expanded to his touch, so the rational part of her mind shrank and receded. In an assault so powerful that she would have sold her soul rather than forgo the experience, emotion and sensation united to banish any shred of timidity she might once have harbored.

Ben kissed her all over, putting his mouth in places that only an hour before would have left her covered with blushes. But where then she might have fought the tide cresting over her, now she abandoned herself to it and cried aloud as it swept her to delirium.

Possessed by the desire to give to him as fully as he gave to her, she rose up to meet him as he knelt above her. He caught her face between his two hands. His eyes, dark and fathomless in the faint light, stared into hers.

Leaning forward, she kissed him on the mouth. He tasted of the body lotion she'd used that morning, of the sweet sea breeze that had filled the car as she sat watching the sun go down and of her, a woman in the full bloom of passion.

She had never loved him as deeply or fiercely as she did at that moment. She would have died for him, if he'd asked her to.

Instead, he steeled himself to patience, the selfless teacher willing to wait as long as it took for her to be ready to progress to the next stage of the journey. It wasn't easy for him, though. That much she could tell from the way he fought to control his labored breathing, and from the film of sweat pearling his brow.

But she'd learned at the hands of a master. Now, she knew how to give, as well as take. Unselfconsciously and intent only on trying to return some of the pleasure with which he'd so generously infused her, she ran her lips down the length of his torso and buried her face against the silken heat of him.

Many times over the course of their courtship, her hints that she wanted him to make love to her had met with enough resistance to make her wonder if she'd ever possess the wherewithal to shatter his impressive control. But his reaction to her brazen assault banished any lingering doubt.

Unschooled she might be, but unappealing—at least to the only person on earth who mattered—she was not! His indrawn breath and the sudden swift pressure of his hand against her skull were not the actions of a man unmoved by a woman. Elated, she reveled in the heat of him, in the reflexive spasm gripping his body, and his harsh utterance of her name.

It was time. She knew it and so did he. When he pulled her up beside him, she came willingly. When he pressed her down against the mattress, she held out her arms to him. When he nudged at her, she opened her legs and accepted him gladly.

She welcomed the momentary pain as he entered her for the reminder it was: that she had saved herself for this moment and this man. It was a small price to pay for the rush of delicious pleasure that followed, for the sense of belonging she could never, in her wildest dreams, have anticipated.

This was what marriage was about. *This* was what formed the charmed circle symbolized by the wedding ring on her finger. As long as they could soar together like this in a world entirely of their own making, *nothing* could come between them.

Winding her arms around his neck, she tried to absorb him more deeply within her, but he surprised her by pulling back. Bracing himself on his arms, he stared down at her and slowing the rhythm of his loving until he was barely moving, withdrew from her almost completely.

''Don't leave me,'' she cried, overwhelmed by an aching sense of loss.

''Never,'' he said huskily, probing deep again in a long, sure sweep. ''I love you, Julia.''

And so it went, with him teasing and provoking her until she was coiled tight as a steel spring and uttering incoherent little pleas for deliverance.

Enslaved, enraptured, enthralled, she savored every tiny torture, hardly aware that a distant trembling was gathering force within her and threatening to shatter her into a million pieces.

Ben sensed it before she did. He froze and for a second, she felt she was teetering on the brink of extinction. Unsure what she was asking for but knowing that she couldn't survive without it, she heard herself whimper, ''Please Ben…!''

''Yes,'' he said, driving hard and furiously in answer to her need. ''Yes!''

Time blurred. Life altered shape. Everything that was familiar shifted to a new focus. Caught up in the unrelenting rhythm, she flew with him in a star burst of ecstasy beyond the boundaries of her previous existence to a new and glorious plane.

Oh, Mother, she thought dazedly, so flooded with scandalous delight that she didn't know how she remained earthbound, *what a lot you must have missed when it comes to being with the man you love!*

She lay beside him, her face flushed and her eyelids still heavy with passion. ''I'm so happy, Ben,'' she murmured, smiling up at him dreamily.

"That's all I've ever wanted for you," he said, and tucked her head into the curve of his shoulder before she picked up on the misgivings a more alert observer would surely have read in his guarded reply.

She snuggled against him, warm and trusting. "I never thought our first time together would be so wonderful."

"Me either."

That much at least was true. In fact, to say their lovemaking had been good was tantamount to regarding Mount Everest as a bit of a steep climb. The words had yet to be invented to do justice to the magnitude of the experience. So that being so, why was he lying there staring bleakly into the night and listening to alarm bells clanging out a warning at the back of his mind?

He knew why. It had all come about too easily. One minute they'd been digging themselves even deeper into the pit of mistrust and disappointment that had defined the parameters of their marriage so far, and the next they'd been rolling around in bed.

To his way of thinking now that sanity prevailed again, that had been nothing less than a case of short-term gain for long-term pain. Sex wasn't the glue that held a relationship together. More likely, it was the thing that fell apart soonest when things began to go wrong. On the other hand, it was a beginning and the place where marriage usually began. Maybe they'd get lucky for a change, and what they'd shared tonight would pave the way for greater understanding in other areas, too.

Smothering a yawn, he punched the pillow more comfortably behind his head and let out a long breath. He couldn't remember when he'd last felt so tired. What with the baby's erratic schedule and the worry gnawing at him every waking moment, he'd barely slept in a week. If he could get in a couple of hours now…

Right on cue, the monitor next to the bed emitted a testy squawk. Julia heard, too, and when he went to climb out of bed, caught at his arm. ''Let me,'' she said.

''No. You don't have to do this, Julia.''

Her silhouette showed in dark relief against the faint light at the window. Naked, graceful, beautiful. Weary as he was, and despite his misgivings, he felt the old familiar ache spreading through his belly.

"I want to," she said.

And I want you, he thought. He would always want her. The question was, could he keep her? Perhaps the answer was at hand. If she could accept the baby, the worst hurdles facing them would surely be over. "Okay. But if you need help, I'm here."

"I can manage," she said. "Get some rest, sweetheart."

More than happy to accommodate her, he fell back against the pillows. He was almost asleep before she was out of the room.

The night-light in the nursery showed the baby, red-faced and furious, flailing the air with his tiny fists. Scooping him out of the crib, Julia patted his little bottom experimentally. "Well, no wonder you're so upset," she crooned. "You're soaked and starving."

Momentarily distracted by the sound of another voice, he stopped crying and regarded her out of huge, unblinking eyes the exact same shade of blue as Ben's.

"Hi," she said softly. "I'm Julia, your... mommy."

If daring to say the word didn't quite produce the miracle she'd hoped for, what happened next came pretty close. As if he'd finally come home, the baby uttered a long, quivering sigh and nuzzled the side of her neck.

Yet again that night, but for vastly different reasons, she felt as if she'd inadvertently touched a live electric wire. The impact of that blindly seeking little mouth rooting against her skin rocked her to the soul. She'd read about women being tigresses when it came to protecting their young, but she'd never expected to experience the feeling firsthand with another woman's baby.

Dear God, she thought, blinking away a sudden haze of tears, *is this what they mean when they talk about maternal instinct?*

"Hang on, sweetie," she murmured, searching through the items stacked on the shelves of the infant change table. "As soon as I find what I need here, we'll be in business."

There were doll-size undershirts, terry-cloth sleepers, a stack of disposable diapers and a bewildering array of accessories to choose from, everything from powder to cream to a carton of little damp towelettes. By the time she'd collected the bare essentials, the baby had grown tired of trying to milk nourishment out of her neck and was giving vent to his annoyance.

"Hush, Squirt," she whispered, popping a pacifier in his mouth and stealing downstairs with him. "Things can only get better from here on in."

In fact, they grew worse. The diaper was prefolded in such a way that she put it on inside out and realized her mistake only when she tried to fasten the adhesive tabs. Frustrated, she started over, but by the time she had him clean and ready to eat, the baby was beside himself.

''We need a rocking chair,'' she said, parking herself on one of the stools at the breakfast bar and offering him his bottle. ''One of those big old things with fat cushions and a high back so that we can be comfortable while we do this. We'll get your daddy onto it first thing in the morning. And we can't go on calling you Squirt forever. We've got to come up with a better name for you, something nice and strong that will still fit when you're all grown up.''

But he'd grown tired of listening to her babble, or else she wasn't holding him right. Why else was he refusing to take the bottle and letting out little cries of distress?

Settling him in the crook of her other arm, she tried again, all the while nattering on as if he understood every word. ''You already have the best daddy in the world, you know, and I'll try to be the best mommy. Even if I have other babies later on, I promise I'll never make you feel left out or different. You'll be their big brother, the one they all look up to.''

But the chatter intended to soothe him, and the milk that should have assuaged his hunger pangs weren't working. Instead of growing contented, he thrashed his head from side to side, stiffened his little limbs and refused to take the bottle even though she'd made sure the temperature was just right.

Maybe it was the way she was holding him, scrunched up on her lap and sandwiched between her and the breakfast bar. Maybe if she rocked him a little…

"I know what it is," she said, jiggling him in her arms as she paced the floor. "Too much has happened to you, too many strangers have come in and out of your life, and you're scared. But you're home to stay now, sweetie pie, and you'll never be abandoned again."

Still, nothing she did or said worked. Weakly, he pushed away the bottle. When she foolishly tried to force him to taste the milk, he choked on it and what he'd managed to take down came shooting back up again. After he'd regained his breath, he started to cry. Really cry, with real tears puddling down his face.

They were contagious. Desperate to console him, she said, her voice breaking, ''I'm new at this, but I'm doing my best, really I am. I've never had any practice in the baby department, you know. In fact, yours is the first diaper I've ever changed. Is that the trouble? Can you tell I don't really know what I'm doing?''

He answered with a mighty howl. It didn't raise the dead, but it brought Ben staggering downstairs wearing nothing but his briefs, and with his hair all awry and his eyes slitted with fatigue.

''Oh, Ben, I don't know what I'm doing wrong!'' she wailed, the tears pressing hot behind her eyes because here she was, failing him once more, and so soon after they'd found each other again.

He squinted at the baby. ''Don't take it personally,'' he said. ''He's the same with me, most of the time. I guess he knows we're not really up to speed on this parenting thing.''

''He's *not* the same with you,'' she said. ''I've never heard him scream like this when you're looking after him. I think he knows I tried to ignore him at first so now he won't accept me because he doesn't trust me.'' She sniffled pathetically. ''Maybe he never will. Maybe I'm not cut out for motherhood.''

Ben plucked the baby from her arms, parked him in his infant seat on the counter and gave the bottle another try. ''Maybe,'' he said, snaring her with his free arm and reeling her close, ''you're expecting too much, too soon. Miracles don't happen overnight, honey.''

That he could still call her ''honey,'' even when the best she could do was reduce his son to howling rage, and hold her pressed close to his side as he juggled the bottle, gave her new hope.

''How can you tell what a baby needs?'' she said, wrapping her arms around his waist and inhaling the lovely male, sleep-warm scent of his bare skin. ''I changed his diaper and gave him clean jammies before I fed him. What did I miss?''

Laughter rumbled deep in Ben's chest. ''Jammies, Julia?'' he inquired. ''Good grief, woman, no wonder he's raising the roof! Don't you know we men don't go for that kind of baby talk? We like our language straight up.''

''He's not a man,'' she said, peering anxiously at the child. ''He's just an itty-bitty baby and he was very unhappy with me. Why do you think he throws up so much?''

''I don't know,'' Ben said, dropping a slow, sweet kiss on her mouth. ''But when I spoke to Marian earlier, she said that—''

A second before, Julia had been suffused with warmth and optimism. But the words he so casually dropped chilled her to the bone. Images of Marian Dawes came to mind. Pretty, petite Marian; helpless, clinging Marian, too weak to stand on her own two feet and willing to settle for any kind of marriage rather than no marriage at all. Willing to give up her infant son for a man who was, at best, an unfeeling brute.

Why was she in touch with Ben now? Had the deal she'd brokered with her bullying husband turned sour so soon? Was she regretting giving up her baby for him?

It was the kitten business all over again. Just when she let her guard down, the thing Julia most yearned for was about to be snatched away from her. ''You spoke to Marian?'' she said, striving for calm. ''Did *she* call *you?*''

If he hadn't noticed the way she stiffened in his embrace, then stepped away from him, surely he heard the touch-me-not tone in her voice? But lifting the baby out of the seat and hoisting him on his shoulder, Ben said easily, ''No. I phoned her.''

''When?'' she said, sidling behind the other side of the breakfast bar before she forgot herself and went to pull his hair out by the roots.

''Earlier this evening, while you were out.''

''You phoned her? And then you made love to me?''

''I don't see the connection between the two, *Julia.*''

His sudden watchfulness, and the way he paced his answer, with a clearly defined pause between each word, were a warning in themselves to watch how she responded, but she was long past caring. ''My point exactly,

Benjamin! There shouldn't *be* any connection. She belongs in the past. At least, that's what you gave me to understand when you begged me not to walk out on our wedding. So why would you deliberately invite her into our lives now?''

''Because I needed advice. You might not have noticed until tonight that this child isn't your average happy baby, but I've been wrestling with the knowledge for nearly a week. And as his father, I am concerned.''

''That still doesn't explain why you'd turn to Marian Dawes.''

''It doesn't? I'd have thought it was obvious. She's his mother.''

She's his mother…!

And you, Julia, will never be more than a substitute, no matter how much you try to fool yourself into believing otherwise!

''And you'd give credence to the opinion of a woman who turned her back on her own baby? Come on, Ben, you can surely do better than that! What's the real reason you wanted to talk to your former mistress?''

"Well, until tonight, you hadn't shown any interest in him, so who do you suggest I should have turned to? Your mother?" He snorted derisively. "Hell, I'd as soon put my faith in a rabid pit bull!"

"You could have asked my grandmother."

"No, I couldn't. Because doing so would have revealed how little support I was getting from you and I'm too fond of Felicity to want to be the one to destroy her illusions about her only grandchild."

"Are you suggesting—?"

"What I'm suggesting," he said wearily, "is that we can this conversation right now before we both wind up saying things we'll live to regret. I'm tired, you're tired and God knows this baby should be tired. So let's put the matter on hold until we've all had some rest."

And without giving her the chance to argue the point, he turned and walked out of the room. She had never felt more lonely in her life.

CHAPTER SEVEN

SHE had not thought she'd so soon pass yet another sleepless night. Even less had she imagined it would take place in the guest room. But when she finally followed Ben upstairs, the door to the master suite was closed and it took more stamina than she possessed to intrude on its lone occupant, even if he was now her husband in every sense of the word.

The baby stirred as she passed by the nursery. Tiptoeing to the crib, she stooped to twitch the satin-bound quilt in place and stroked her hand over his face and head. His hair was damp with sweat and he seemed warmer than she'd have thought was normal.

Had she judged Ben too harshly? Was there something more wrong with this little mite than a bad case of colic or whatever it was that had him drawing his knees up to his stomach so often? Were the bruises his father had noticed an indication of a more serious condition?

A thread of fear rippled up her spine. Babies weren't any different from other people. Dreadful illness could strike without warning. They could die.

He whimpered in his sleep and sucked fiercely on his pacifier, and she knew a sudden need to pick him up and hold him close, as much to ward off any hovering evil as to let him know that all the anger she'd spewed out in the kitchen hadn't been directed at him.

But she hated to disturb him so she touched her fingertip to the petal-soft skin of his cheek instead. ''I could so easily fall in love with you, if I dared,'' she whispered, a sudden tear spilling down her face and splashing onto his. ''But it's not that simple, you see.''

''Yes, it is,'' Ben said, and she spun around to find him standing behind her. ''It's every bit as simple as that, Julia. All you have to do is stop fighting and let it happen.''

As flustered as if she'd been caught stealing, she snatched back her hand and straightened. ''I didn't mean to wake you.''

"I wasn't sleeping," he said. "And even if I had been, the monitor beside the bed is so sensitive that I can hear him breathing. I knew the minute you came in here."

He yawned and shook his head vigorously, as if doing that would be enough to bring the rest of his six feet plus fully alert. Coming to stand beside her, he looked down at his son. "How's he doing?"

"Well, he's sleeping. I guess that's a good sign. But if he were my child—"

"He is your child, Julia, if you want him to be."

"No," she said. "He's Marian's. You said so yourself not half an hour ago." Then, seeing the way his mouth tightened and his chest rose in an impatient sigh, she hurried on, "But if he were mine, I'd be taking him to a doctor for a thorough checkup."

"I'm way ahead of you. I've got an appointment with a pediatrician first thing Monday morning."

"That's a long time to wait, especially if there's something really wrong with him."

''I know. That's why I phoned Marian. I figured that if she hadn't noticed anything in the month that he was with her, whatever's bugging him now probably isn't too serious.''

''Well then,'' she said, turning away from the crib, ''if you and she are in agreement about how you should handle matters, what I think is neither here nor there, is it?''

He caught up with her just outside the door and she knew from his firm grasp on her elbow that the conversation was far from over. ''You're being very silly about this Marian business, you know,'' he said, as if he were talking to a four-year-old.

''And you're being unbelievably obtuse if you can't understand that the last name I want to hear coming out of your mouth is Marian Dawes! Isn't it enough that there are three of us on this so-called honeymoon, without your inviting a fourth along, as well?''

''That's a bit over the top, even for you, Julia.''

''No, it's not,'' she said, rounding on him. ''The woman's been in my face practically from the minute you and I said our 'I do's.' And just when I thought we might be getting past at least some of the misery she's caused, you have to bring her back to center stage with a phone call—and even worse, do it while my back's turned.''

''What would you have preferred? That I waited until you decided to show up again, and make it a conference call?''

''That kind of sarcasm is uncalled for.''

Arms folded, he rocked back and forth on his heels. The look in his eyes was that of a stranger. ''You're right,'' he said. ''On every count. I'm a schmuck, she's a bitch and you're a saint. So what do I have to do to set things right, Julia? Have her arrested and thrown in jail? Walk over hot coals? Wear a hair shirt?''

''How can you be so blind?'' she cried, the confounded tears spurting forth again. It seemed to her that she'd cried more in the last week than she had in her previous twenty-three years. Was there never to be an end to it? ''Can't you see that I'm scared of her? She's given you a son. She's a big part of your past.

And she's a fool because she left you for a jerk who'll end up breaking her heart and probably her spirit, too. And when that happens, she's likely to decide she wants both her baby and his father back in her life.''

She dashed away the tears and gave an almighty sniff. ''When you asked me to marry you, I assumed it was because you felt the same way I did—that you couldn't live without me. I never expected I'd feel redundant before I'd even taken off my wedding dress!''

She wouldn't have believed that in baring her deepest fears, she'd move him so profoundly, both literally and figuratively. Before she could catch her breath, he'd snatched her up and was carrying her into the bedroom, *their* bedroom, and was murmuring into her hair—lovely, healing things, like, ''Sweetheart, I'm sorry.… I'm an ass.… I didn't mean to make you cry. Don't ever think I'd leave you—not for Marian, not for any woman…it'll never happen. I give you my solemn promise it'll never happen.''

''But what if she put you in the position of having to choose between keeping the baby or being with me?'' she sobbed, able at last to air every last ghost that had haunted her so relentlessly over the past week.

''It'll never happen,'' he said again, tipping her face up to his and mopping up her tears with tiny, tender kisses. ''I won't let it. How can I make you believe that?''

''Keep her away from us,'' she said, burying her face in his shoulder. ''I'm trying to build the happy family you want, Ben, but it's not easy. Asking me to accept your baby's one thing, but to expect me to welcome his mother into our lives is too much. Promise me you won't let her come anywhere near us, ever again.''

She knew what his answer would be even before he leaned away from her and cupping her chin in his hand, said, ''I'll try to keep her at a distance, Julia, but that's about the best I can do at this point.''

''I don't know if I can live with that kind of uncertainty hanging over my head all the time,'' she said.

He sandwiched her hands between his and squeezed them. "Honey," he said, "in light of everything that's gone down in the last few days, I know I'm asking a lot when I say please trust me to handle this. Marian's made some pretty major mistakes, no doubt about it, but she's basically decent and I don't think she's going to be a problem, at least nothing that you and I can't deal with as long as we stick together. But you're right. She's made a pact with the devil and his name's Wayne Dawes. In light of what we already know about him, not to mention what I suspect, I'm taking steps to make sure there's not the slightest chance he'll ever be an influence in my son's life."

He sounded so confident, so in charge, that she wanted to believe him. "What kind of steps?"

"I'm suing for full legal custody of the baby. Given her attachment to Dawes, I don't imagine Marian's going to fight me on it, but until the papers have been signed, I'm not about to do anything to stir things up between us. Sole custody isn't often granted these days. In the interests of the child, it's usually shared between both parents. But in this case, I want the courts to look favorably on both you and me to the point that there's no question but that we are what's best for that little boy.''

''And what if she won't agree to give you sole legal custody? What if she wants visitation rights and shows up on our doorstep whenever the spirit moves her?'' The specter of Marian Dawes being a permanent fixture in their lives was enough to start her weeping again. ''What if—?''

He reached over to a box of tissues on the bedside table and tugged a fistful free to dab at her tears. ''Honey,'' he said, ''I don't pretend to have all the answers but I'm working on them. Right now, though, I'm beat and so are you. Please let's call it a day and talk about this again when we've had some rest. Things always look better in the morning.''

''I'll never be able to sleep,'' she howled.

"Yes, you will. Here, blow." He pinched the end of her nose lightly with a fresh tissue. "That's better. Now go take a nice long bath while I fix us a drink, then come to bed with me."

He steered her down the hall to the room she'd occupied since the day they'd moved into the house. During the half hour she spent in the tub, he made good use of the time at his disposal. When she showed up at his door again, all shining and smelling of flowers, he'd changed the sheets, turned the lamps down low, taken a shower and was waiting with a glass of hot milk for her and a snifter of brandy for himself.

"Personally," he said, hauling her into bed beside him and passing over the glass, "I'd rather drink antifreeze, but I believe hot milk's the preferred remedy for helping a person relax, especially if it's spiked with a shot of brandy."

What with her dark hair spread out on the pillows piled up behind her, and her demure cotton nightshirt that left her arms and neck bare but covered up everything else, she looked about fourteen years old. The thought didn't exactly give Ben comfort. The difference in their ages had always troubled him, but never more so than in the last few days.

Sure, she had a certain sophistication about her. Given her upbringing, it followed that she would. But her life had been sheltered, too, and he'd known that to expect that she'd simply take in her stride the bombshell that had landed in her lap on their wedding day, was absurd. He'd believed, though, that in time, she'd come to accept his son, and all indications were that he'd been right. But now another, potentially more damaging problem had surfaced and that, he feared, wasn't going to be so easily resolved.

Beside him, she slumped over her hot milk, then snapped her head up again with a start. ''I think you're just about gone,'' he said, removing the half-empty glass from her hand.

''I think you're right,'' she said. ''The brandy cocktail did the trick.''

She sighed sleepily, then slithered down under the covers, snuggled up next to him and slung her arm across his hips. Without being too obvious about it, he moved her hand out of the danger zone. He didn't relish making love to an unconscious woman but nor was he made of stone, and the memory of how she'd felt, all silky and tight around him when they made love, was enough all by itself to get him revved up again. He could do without her accidentally touching him in his most susceptible area and adding dynamite to the mix. Sex, though undeniably enjoyable, wasn't the answer to the problems facing them.

Her breathing slowed and became more regular. He turned off the lamp and leaned against the headboard in the dark, sipping his brandy and trying to figure out how they were going to avoid the pitfalls that lay ahead. He'd more or less fobbed her off with a sugarcoated version of the truth, but there was no use in trying to fool himself. Even a successful bid for custody wasn't going to make Marian disappear in a puff of smoke.

She was the baby's mother and that made her as much a fact of the future as she was of the past and the present. He wished it weren't so, but wishing didn't change a damn thing.

The next afternoon, Felicity stopped by. "I won't come in," she said, when he opened the door, "I just wanted to drop off some of the wedding gifts. I thought you could both use a change of pace from what you've been dealing with lately, and opening presents is always fun, as long as you don't end up with fourteen different electric mixers."

"You're coming in," he said, ushering her firmly over the threshold. "Do you really think we'd let you drive all the way out here and not at least offer you something to drink?"

"Well…" She dropped him a sly wink. "I have to admit I wouldn't mind taking a peek at that sweet baby of yours, just for a minute."

"That sweet baby, Felicity, has kept us up all night, every night, for the last week!"

"They're inclined to do that," she said placidly. "And if they're not keeping you up with their fussing, you're lying there wide awake anyway, wondering if they're still breathing. It's the nature of the little beasts, Ben, but we love them regardless. How's my granddaughter doing, by the way?''

She was too wise to be fooled by half truths. ''It's touch and go,'' he admitted in a low voice. ''Frankly, I thank God for each day that I get up and find her still here.''

''Having a new baby in the house is a strain even under the best of circumstances, you know. Her father howled for the entire first three months of his life. I remember being ready to throw him out of the window on occasion.'' She gave another droll wink. ''I'd have thrown myself out as well, except we lived in a rancher and it wouldn't have done me any good!''

It had been so long since he laughed that the muscles in his face ached. ''Don't say things like that in front of Julia. You might give her ideas!''

''She's not bonding with the baby?''

"He's not the problem so much as the baggage he comes with. She and I need to sit down and talk quietly, without distraction. But trying to do that around here is damn near impossible."

Felicity eyed him thoughtfully. "When was the last time the two of you had time alone together?"

The question caught him off guard. "Come to think of it," he said, scratching his head, "I can't remember."

"Then I'm very glad I invited myself over," she said briskly. "Tell your bride you're taking her out for dinner tonight, Ben. I'll stay here and hold down the fort while you're gone."

"I can't ask you to do that. You don't know what you'll be taking on."

She rolled her eyes. "Dear boy, have you forgotten the daughter-in-law I'm saddled with? Compared to Stephanie, your little son will be a piece of cake, even for an old bird like me! Now take me to my granddaughter. I want her to give me a tour of this lovely home you've given her.''

He had to turn away before he made a fool of himself. Damn it, she just about had him in tears with her warmth. He hadn't felt so completely accepted or approved of in years, not since he was a kid of eight or nine. ''If she divorces me,'' he said thickly, ''will you still be my friend?''

''She will divorce you,'' Felicity said sternly, ''over my dead body. And since only the good are supposed to die young, I'll be around for a good many years yet. As for being your friend, it goes without saying and I'm surprised you'd even have to ask. You are part of my family, Ben, and I love you.''

He choked and tried to cover it up with a cough. ''The two don't always follow.''

''I know that better than most, my dear. But in your case, they are inseparable.''

He managed to get them a table on the rooftop terrace of a new French restaurant on the beachfront. What with the potted palm trees and clay planters stuffed to overflowing with brightly colored flowers, and the brilliant blue of sea and sky, they might have been dining on the Riviera.

"Well?" He smiled at Julia. She'd put her hair up and had on a pale blue summer suit with pearl buttons. She looked stunning, the way a week-old bride should. Almost. Her answering smile was a little too tentative, her eyes not quite as clear and untroubled as he'd have liked.

"It's lovely," she said, looking around.

"So are you, sweetheart," he replied, and wished he could guarantee she'd still be blushing with pleasure at the evening's end.

He fed her smoked breast of duck, poached pear salad and fat prawns in Pernod, all washed down with champagne. By the time the crême brulée she ordered for dessert arrived, she'd relaxed enough to let her guard down— not something she'd allowed to happen too often in the days since the wedding.

He waited until then before approaching the one topic of conversation he'd been putting on hold all day. Sneaky, no doubt, by most people's standards, but to his way of thinking, extraordinary difficulties called for extraordinary solutions.

Reaching for her hand, he stroked his thumb over the bright new gold of her wedding ring and searched for a casually diplomatic lead-in. "You're going to be a wonderful mother, honey. Marian's lucky you were there to take over when she decided she wasn't up for the job. And speaking of Marian—"

In a flash, the wariness was back in her eyes. Her hand, which had lain warm and pliant beneath his, turned rigid as stone. "I didn't know we were," she said. "In fact, I can't imagine why you'd even bring her into the conversation, particularly since you were so insistent that we have this time all to ourselves."

Well, so much for biding his time and mincing his words! He might just as well have stated his case baldly at breakfast and shot the entire day to hell!

Too much of what he was thinking must have shown on his face. Zeroing in on it,

Julia's gaze narrowed. ''Or was softening Julia up with wine so that she'd be more amenable to your agenda what tonight was all about to begin with?''

He swallowed and looked away. There was too much truth in her allegation for him to bring himself to refute it, and she recognized that, too.

''Well!'' She flung down her napkin and snatched up her purse. ''Here's a news flash, Ben. It'll take a lot more than a few swigs of champagne to make me toe this particular party line. Your son is one thing. Your ex-lover is another. I *will not* tolerate sharing my marriage with her. So make up your mind who you want and do it fast before I find myself in any deeper than I already am.''

''Meaning what?'' he said, grabbing her hand to keep her from walking out on him.

Her eyes glowed like coals in the flickering light of the hurricane lamp on the table. ''Meaning I'm not about to invest any more of myself in you or your baby until I know for sure I'm not going to wind up empty-handed.

You've taken enough away from me—my trust, the kind of future I thought we faced, the sort of happiness I thought we were guaranteed when you asked me to marry you. I'm not going to wait until you break my heart over that little boy before I cut my losses. So have a drink on that, Ben Carreras, and damn well let go of my hand before I make a scene you won't soon forget!''

He didn't have much choice, at least on the latter. With a flick of her wrist, she wrenched herself free and left him alone to face an audience of other diners enthralled by the impromptu entertainment of seeing a guy dumped by his date for the evening.

''Cheers!'' he said, lifting his glass in scornful response. ''Here's looking up your old address, folks!''

She walked home, taking the nearly deserted brick-paved sea walk, then following the curve of the beach so that there was no chance he'd pull up beside her in the car and demand that she ride with him. She'd sooner have flown on a broomstick, which he no doubt was beginning to think was where she belonged.

But right at that moment, she didn't care what he thought. Right at that moment, she hated him, and she couldn't understand why admitting it made her start crying all over again.

A middle-aged couple out for a late stroll under the stars passed her and seeing her distress, stopped. "Do you need help?" the woman asked.

Such kindly concern from a stranger who owed her nothing completely undid Julia. Overcome, she shook her head and hurried on.

Her grandmother stood at the open front door when she arrived home. "Heavenly nights, Julia, here you are at last!"

By then thoroughly composed again, she said, "I gather that Ben's already here and has told you what a wonderful evening we had."

"He's been and gone again, child," Felicity said.

"Gone?" she echoed blankly, feeling as if her legs were about to fold under her. How was it that one man could put a woman through such a maelstrom of emotion? How was it possible to hate him one moment and be terrified that she'd lost him, the next?

"He took the baby to the hospital."

"Hospital?"

Felicity clicked her tongue impatiently. "Is there something amiss with your hearing, Julia, that you find it necessary to repeat everything I say as if you're not sure you understood me correctly? Ben has taken the baby to the Peace Arch Hospital. The child is very ill. His father is extremely upset and worried. So am I, and I would be with both of them now, but you chose to go missing. So I stayed here instead, because your husband was concerned about where you'd got to and he didn't want you coming home to an empty house. Personally, I think that man has enough on his plate, without having to sweat over the fact that his wife's disappeared yet again, but I suspect my opinion carries little weight with you these days."

"If you're determined to lay blame," Julia replied, stung, "blame Ben! He's the one at fault this time, not me."

Her grandmother didn't reply to that, but the glance she turned on her was so loaded with disappointment that Julia hardly knew where to look. ''I suppose you think that's hardly important right now,'' she muttered.

''Do *you* think it is, my angel?''

''No,'' she said, feeling about ten years old again. ''The baby's health is all that matters. Will you...come with me to the hospital, Amma?''

''No,'' Felicity said. ''As long as he has you by his side, Ben doesn't need me. But if you don't mind, I'd like to stay here until the morning. Not only do I want to hear how my great-grandson's doing as soon as possible, but my night vision isn't what it used to be and I don't feel comfortable driving in the dark. I won't put you out at all. I'll be perfectly comfortable on the couch.''

Stricken, Julia saw the toll the evening had taken on her grandmother's energy. Fatigue and worry had her looking every one of her seventy-nine years. ''You'll do no such thing!'' she exclaimed, steering her toward the staircase. "Take the guest room at the end of the hall—the one overlooking the back garden. The bed's already made up and you'll find everything you need in the bathroom."

Ben's car was in the parking area outside the hospital when she arrived, but he was nowhere to be found in the emergency room. "The Carreras baby?" the nurse said, when Julia inquired. "Oh, he had to be shipped to Children's in Vancouver."

"For colic?" Julia's breath snagged with sudden fear. "Why couldn't he be looked after here?"

"Unless you're the mother, I'm afraid I can't give you any more information, ma'am."

Was she the mother? It was the question she'd put off facing until another day, until a time when the stressful emotional baggage that had cluttered her marriage to date had been dealt with. Except, suddenly, today was now, and there was no more procrastinating.

"Not exactly," she said. "But he's my husband's son and I'm...I'm his stepmother."

Stepmother! Julia's voice broke on the word. What a cold, unfeeling image to attach to such a tiny, helpless baby!

''I think that qualifies.'' The nurse reached for a folder on the desk. ''His little tummy was very distended and our medical team suspect he might need surgery. They weren't about to take a chance on it—we don't have the facilities here—so they flew him to Children's.''

''*Flew* him?''

''By helicopter. His father went with him. They left about half an hour ago.''

''But to fly him, when it takes less than an hour to drive! Is it *so* serious?''

The nurse regarded her sympathetically. ''He's very young, Mrs. Carreras. We can't afford to adopt a wait-and-see approach with babies his age. To do so could be life-threatening.''

''Oh, God!'' She clapped a hand to her mouth to stifle the sudden sob that erupted. Not all the tears she'd shed over the last week amounted to a drop in the ocean of despair and dismay that overwhelmed her then.

"I'm sorry, Mrs. Carreras, I didn't mean to frighten you. All I'm trying to point out is that if surgery is necessary, he'll receive the best possible care at Children's, so try not to worry." The nurse came around the desk and put an arm around Julia's shoulders. "I'm a mother myself, and that's easy advice to dispense and just about impossible to follow, I know."

"I have to go to him," Julia whispered, the horror of the whole business washing over her afresh. What was it about her and Ben that their every step forward was followed by two steps back? And why did a baby have to be caught up in the middle of all the ugliness?

CHAPTER EIGHT

SHE found him in the waiting room on the sur-
gical floor at Children's Hospital. He sat at one
end of a couch, head bowed, hands hanging
loosely between his knees and such an air of
despair about him that her own heart failed.

"Ben?" She touched him on the shoulder.
"Is there any news?"

"No."

"Did they say how long…?"

"No."

"When did they take him in?"

"An hour ago—forty minutes." He lifted
one shoulder in a shrug. "I wasn't watching
the clock."

"Do they know what's wrong?"

"They've got a pretty good idea."

"And they can fix it?" She ached to take
him in her arms but he'd so thoroughly iso-
lated himself in his own private world of mis-

192

ery that she dared not. Instead, she sat beside him on the couch and begged, ''Talk to me, Ben, please. Don't shut me out.''

He lifted his head long enough to fix her in a long stare. His blue eyes, so startling in contrast to his dark, Spanish-American beauty, illuminated his face with a cool, clear light that had always seemed able to look past all the external nonsense to the real heart of any matter.

They dissected her now with unforgiving candor and a weariness that had nothing to do with fatigue. ''Sorry, Julia, but I'm about talked out and I'm sure as hell not up to going another round with you. So do us both a favor and go home.''

''No,'' she said, covering his hand with hers as if that would stop him from slipping out of reach forever. ''If I didn't know it before, I learned tonight that walking away doesn't help anything. He's my baby, too, Ben. Not legally, perhaps, but in every way that really counts, and you're my husband. I belong here with you and with him, and whether you like it or not, I'm staying.''

He stared off into the distance. ''I could change your mind real fast on that, Julia.''

''How?'' she said, her skin pebbling with an apprehension unrelated to the drama taking place in the operating room down the hall.

''I called Marian again. It was the first thing I did after they'd taken our son into surgery.''

Strange how the news struck a different nerve from the one it would have attacked three hours ago. Suddenly *I called Marian* didn't assume near the same threatening proportions as *our son.*

Whose son are you referring to? she wanted to ask him. *Yours and mine, or yours and Marian's?*

Accurately gauging her silence for the dismay it represented, he said, ''I sense the volcano is about to erupt. Well, don't hold back on my account, just go find somewhere else to do it. Oh, yeah, and one more thing. Don't expect me to come crawling after you begging forgiveness for my crass insensitivity to your finer feelings because it's not going to happen. Marian had a right to know our child's ill and I had an obligation to tell her.''

''Let's not fight about Marian,'' Julia said urgently. ''Right now, we should be focusing all our energy on your son. He needs our strength, our love, to help him pull through this. Because, if he should die—'' she swallowed the sudden lump in her throat as the unthinkable reared up to confront her ''—it will destroy us, Ben. Our marriage will be over.''

''Is that all he is to you—a passport to marriage?'' he said, bleak disgust coating his words with ice.

''Of course not! That isn't...!'' Horrified that he could even *think* her capable of such blatant self-interest, she clapped a hand to her mouth.

''That's what it sounded like to me.''

''What I meant,'' she said, her voice trembling, ''is he's part of us, part of the very heart of our marriage. Without him, something vital will be missing.''

"Couples do survive such tragedies. It has been known to happen, if they're both pulling together."

"But we've had so much to deal with already and people can take only so much before they break. I don't want us to break, Ben."

"You could have fooled me. The way you've acted at times, this last week—"

"But it has been only *one* week, Ben. Not such a long time for me to absorb the changes I've had thrust on me." She touched his arm pleadingly. "When everything first came out on our wedding day, you asked me to cut you some slack, to show some understanding, and I've tried to do that. Is it too much to ask that you show me a little patience?"

"I've been patient, Julia. I've made allowances. But it hasn't done me much good."

"I'm sorry if I've disappointed you," she said stiffly, annoyed despite herself by his unbending attitude. "Perhaps if I'd known ahead of time how our wedding day would turn out, I could have rehearsed the part you assigned to me. Unfortunately, none of the bridal etiquette manuals I read covered how to respond to the groom handing his wife the unexpected wedding gift of a baby he'd fathered with someone else.''

Whether or not he'd have replied to that she never learned because just then the surgeon came into the room. "Mr. and Mrs. Carreras? I'm Dr. Burns. I operated on Michael and you'll be happy to know he came through everything beautifully. It was pyloric stenosis, just as we suspected from the ultrasound.''

Julia expected Ben to ask questions but he stood there as unresponsive as if he were in a trance, so she said, ''Is he going to be all right, Doctor?''

''Barring complications—which, by the way, I don't anticipate—he should make a full recovery and you'll be taking home a much happier baby than the one you brought in tonight. He's had a rough ride so far, but the worst is over.''

''May we see him?''

''For a minute or two, sure. But he's catching up on his sleep and from the looks of the pair of you, I recommend you do the same. You'll all be in more of a party mood tomorrow.''

He led them through a pair of swing doors to a big window looking into the recovery room. White-knuckled, Ben stared through the pane of glass at the tiny figure hooked up to oxygen and IV tubes on the other side. Julia wasn't sure, but she thought his eyes misted at the sight.

''He's tough like his daddy, Ben,'' she said, clasping his hand. ''He's going to be just fine.''

''He has to be,'' he said brokenly, gripping her fingers as if they were all that held him together.

She heard the heartfelt anguish in his voice and when he looked at her, she saw the full extent of his suffering in his eyes. Wordlessly, she lifted his hand and kissed it.

''You once asked how I'd feel if he turned out not to be mine,'' he said. ''I didn't know the answer then, but I do now. I love him— no strings attached.''

They left soon after, with Julia driving. She waited until they'd cleared the city limits and had picked up speed along the straight, deserted stretch of highway heading south to White Rock before asking, "When did you decide to call him Michael?"

"When they admitted him to the hospital and I had to fill out a whole bunch of forms."

"I didn't know you'd even thought about names," she said, striving to control the hurt she couldn't quite suppress. She'd hoped they'd choose one together.

"I hadn't until tonight when it struck me that, for all that I talked about accepting him as my son, in fact I'd done nothing to prove it. I'd given him nothing. To all intents and purposes, he was just John Doe, currently residing at my address."

"You gave him a home in the real sense of the word, Ben," she said gently. "You opened your arms and your heart to him. That means a whole lot more than just giving him a name. You're a wonderful father."

He slumped in his seat. ''If I'm so wonderful,'' he said bitterly, ''how come I didn't clue in to the fact that there was more to what was going on with him than colic?''

''How were you supposed to know? You're new at this. We both are.''

''That's no excuse. It's my job to look out for him. His survival depends on that and I let him down.''

''Stop blaming yourself,'' she said. ''You're human, just like the rest of us. You—''

But he cut her off with a slash of his hand. ''Stop trying to sugarcoat the truth, Julia,'' he said, turning his face away. ''We both know that if I hadn't spent so much time trying to keep you happy, I might have realized sooner that he needed medical attention.''

After that wounding observation, he didn't acknowledge her presence again for the rest of the trip. In fact, he couldn't have excluded her more effectively if he'd opened the car door and shoved her out onto the side of the road. She simply ceased to exist for him.

Felicity must have heard the car pull up outside. Even though they'd called to give her the good news on the baby's condition before they left the hospital, when they let themselves into the house, she was waiting at the foot of the stairs, her face a study in loving concern.

Without a word, Ben walked into her arms and took from her the comfort Julia had so badly wanted to give him. More vulnerable than she'd ever seen him, he rested his chin against her grandmother's head and let loose with a long, heartbroken sigh.

"Well, dear boy," Felicity said, stroking his hair, "it's been a long, trying night but it's over, that little boy's going to be just fine, thank God, and we've all survived. Go to bed now and sleep late tomorrow with an easy mind because I'll here to take any phone calls that come in."

Watching, and finding herself yet again on the outside looking in, Julia felt all the old resentment churning around inside. This time, though, the anger was directed at herself. What right had she to carp about his having broken her trust when she was guilty of the same sin toward him?

She'd promised before God to support her husband through all adversity and in the short span of their marriage, had broken her word time and again. Small wonder that when he really needed someone, it wasn't to her that he'd turn. Why would he when she was never there for him?

Quietly, she slipped down the hall to the kitchen and stood at the window, watching the glimmering reflection of the pier lights on the water and listening for one of those little sounds to which her ear had become so finely attuned. But the house was wrapped in the dense silence of the post-midnight hours and there was no baby upstairs trying to convey to those in charge that all was not well with him. Ben was right; they had both failed in their parental duties.

After a while, when she thought he'd had time to fall asleep, she followed him upstairs, to the room they'd shared only one other time. She went there not because she thought he'd welcome her into his bed, but because her grandmother occupied the only other furnished bedroom in the house.

But Ben wasn't there, although the clothes he'd been wearing lay strewn across a chair. She found him in the nursery, clad in a pair of pajama bottoms and staring at the empty crib. He looked somehow incomplete without that little body held against his broad chest, and so bereft that it was more than she could do not to go to him. Even if he rejected her, she at least had to try to let him know she was there if he needed her.

For a minute or two, she simply stood next to him, but fatigue had him almost swaying on his feet and when she slipped her arm around his waist, he didn't object. Docile as a sleep-walker, he let her lead him to his own room and his own bed. Without a murmur, he let her pull the covers over him and turn out the lamp before she went into the bathroom to undress and brush her teeth.

She hoped he'd have dropped off to sleep when she returned, but knew from his utter stillness that he was staring into the dark with wide-awake eyes. Cautiously, she slipped into bed next to him, aching to touch him, to kiss him—not in the hope of stirring him to passion but because she wanted so badly to absorb some of his pain and make it her own. But he'd drawn that formidable shell of reserve around him and it was more than she dared to try to penetrate it.

Eventually she drifted off herself, only to awake just before dawn with her head at an awkward angle and her neck aching. He was lying on his side and facing her, with his arm flung across her shoulders. She didn't know if he'd deliberately put it there or if it happened without his knowing while he was sleeping, but she knew that, stiff neck notwithstanding, she'd rather die than try to move and risk having him withdraw it.

Felicity was already up and about when he staggered downstairs the next morning. The table in the breakfast area was set for three and the aroma of freshly brewed coffee, underscored with the bittersweet pungency of freshly squeezed orange juice, filled the air.

"Is that the time?" he croaked, peering at the clock on the wall in shock. "Cripes, I've got to phone the hospital!"

"I already did, dear," Felicity said, busily whisking eggs in a bowl. "Michael is doing wonderfully well and has been moved to a room on the regular ward. You can go in to see him any time but the nurse did say that if you could bring yourself to wait until after eleven, it makes it easier for the staff to get done everything that has to be done. I'm making omelets, by the way, so what would you like in yours? You've got the choice of cheese, onion or mushroom."

Last night, he couldn't have swallowed a crumb but suddenly, in the bright optimistic light of this new morning and with his son on the road to recovery, he was ravenous. "I'll take all three, thanks just the same."

She smiled. "Good. You were getting them anyway."

What an elegant, gracious woman she was. "How'd you manage to look so glamorous first thing in the day, Felicity?" he said. "It's not as if you expected to be sleeping over when you stopped by yesterday, yet here you are with not a hair out of place. I can see where Julia gets her sense of style." He poured himself a cup of coffee and tried to sound casual when he added, "Speaking of Julia, where is she—or didn't she bother to let you know?"

"She's in the garden, cutting roses. Why don't you take your coffee and a cup for her, and have a little visit together while I finish up in here?"

He wasn't sure he wanted a little visit. Last night had finally impressed upon him the futility of trying to get her to accept his past and move on. The sad but simple truth was, she couldn't, for all that she'd been so sympathetically concerned over Michael.

It wasn't her fault and he wasn't trying to shift blame, but perhaps it was time they stopped trying to fool themselves into believing they were going to get the happy ending they'd been so sure was theirs for the taking. However, right then, he didn't have the energy to cope with splitting up, though he was sure, if he asked his mother-in-law for help on the matter, this would be the one time she'd be more than happy to offer advice!

"You can't avoid one another indefinitely, you know," Felicity remarked, watching him from the other side of the breakfast bar.

"I guess not." He shrugged philosophically and topped up his coffee mug. "Wish me luck, Felicity."

He found her at the bottom of the garden where a climbing rose covered with yellow blossoms had run wild over its supporting trellis. When she saw him headed her way, she froze and watched him as warily as if she thought he might produce a shotgun from behind his back and blow her to kingdom come.

"Relax, Julia," he said. "I'm not going to bite you."

Not that he'd mind—she looked good enough to eat! Hair tied up with some sort of white ruffled scarf, skin tanned just enough to look as if it had been dipped in honey, mouth soft and pink and perfect...gad, whoever had said breaking up was hard to do didn't know the half of it!

"I guess you heard that Michael's out of the woods," he said, handing her the coffee.

She nodded and sort of chewed at her lower lip to keep it from quivering. "Yes," she said. "I'm very happy and relieved."

"You don't sound it, and you certainly don't look it. Why the long face, Julia?"

Her glance flickered to a ladybug crawling up her arm. "I know Michael's going to recover. I'm afraid our marriage isn't."

Well, that certainly saved him having to be the one to broach the subject! "I'm afraid you're right," he said gravely.

She made a sound at that, a subdued moan that ripped his heart out. "Don't," he said, resisting the urge to go to her and take her in his arms because, although she needed comfort, he wasn't up to being the one to give it to her, at least not right then. His own emotions were too fragile.

"I wanted us to work out," she said. "I had such high hopes for us, Ben."

He'd never seen her cry before they were married, but since then it seemed to him that was all she'd done, the moments in between were so few and fleeting. This time, though, was different. There were no sobs, no outpourings of frustration or disappointment or needless jealousy. Apart from that one little whimper of distress, she was silent and so were the tears. One at a time, they rolled down her face as smoothly and noiselessly as oil.

"Everyone does, at least in the beginning. Nobody goes into marriage expecting it's going to fall apart on them." He took a mouthful of the scalding coffee and shoved his free hand into his pocket. Anything to keep from going to her, from touching her! "If I'd had any idea of what lay in store for us, I'd never have asked you to marry me in the first place."

"It's my fault—"

"No," he said. "If you're determined to blame someone, blame me. I asked for too much. No man has the right to do that, not to his wife, and not to his marriage."

She wiped her fingers over the tears on her cheek. "If I told you that, for me, the worst is over, would it change your mind about us?"

"Oh, honey," he muttered, swinging away from her before he gave in to the sudden indecision plaguing him, "it's never going to be over, don't you see that?"

"But I love Michael!"

"No, you don't. You *want* to love him, and that's not the same thing."

"You're wrong," she said, and even he had to admit to the conviction in her voice. "Any doubts I might once have had about my feelings for him were resolved last night when I saw him hooked up to all those tubes. If I didn't know it before, I know now that I couldn't love him more if he were my own child. I'm ready to be his mother in every sense of the word, Ben."

"And what about Marian?" He turned to face her again. "Are you ready to accept the fact that she'll always be his birth mother? That I'll never be able to shut her out of our lives completely? That I don't even *want* to do that because it wouldn't be fair to Michael? Can you deal with the possibility that, one day, he's going to want to know about her and that he'll never hear me criticize her or the choices she's made? That I'll teach him that she's a good woman deserving of his respect, his gratitude and, if he's inclined to give it, of his love?"

"I—"

"Wait, Julia, I'm not done!" He cut her off, determined to complete the reality check he'd been trying to avoid. To promote any idea that Marian would just quietly disappear if they looked the other way would be like sticking a Band-Aid on a leaking roof: sooner or later, the whole building would collapse. "How are you going to react when Michael asks if she can come to visit him, or if he can go and spend time with her? What are you going to do if he wants to put the birthday cards she sends next to the ones you gave him? Or if he keeps her picture in his bedroom?

''What if he decides to call her Mother, or Mom? Because all those things could happen, Julia. She might not be the one wiping his nose or kissing it better when he scrapes his knee, or holding the bowl when he throws up, but she'll always be on the perimeter of his life and, by extension, of yours. She's a part of him and I'd never ask him to be ashamed of that, or to disown her because she couldn't raise him herself.''

She sat on the garden bench under the rose arbor and stared at her hands lying folded in her lap. Examined them for so long that he could practically feel his skin pulling inward in anticipation of the blow she'd surely administer if she had a grain of sense. Because he'd used every bit of ammunition in his arsenal to give her good reason to walk away from him in the belief that the best thing for her would be to start over with someone else who didn't have his history. Yet still, a part of him wanted her to stay.

She picked up the roses she'd cut and lifted them to her face. Closed her eyes and inhaled the fragrance. Brushed one soft velvet petal over her cheek. "Are you asking me for a divorce?"

In a flash of perception as inexplicable as déjà vu, he saw how she would look pregnant: calm, dreamy almost, and unbearably beautiful.

But not with your child, buddy! You screwed up too badly before you met her to be the one to father her children. "I think it would be best, yes."

He was on the verge of leaving when she finally spoke. "And what," she said, spilling the roses onto the bench and coming toward him, "if I won't give you one? What if I were to tell you that I've already come to the same realization about Marian and accepted all those points you just mentioned?"

"They're easy words to say, Julia, but tough to abide by."

"Well, here's something even tougher. I'll agree to a divorce if you can look me in the eye and tell me you're no longer in love with me. And that is the *only* reason I'm going to walk away from this marriage."

"Oh, for Pete's sake, Julia!"

"Never mind Pete. This isn't about him, it's about you and me. So go ahead, Ben. Let me have it. Heaven knows I've given you reason enough to decide you can live without me and nobody who knows you is going to think any less of you for cutting your losses before they get any worse."

"I can't say it. You know damned well I can't."

Her smile put the sun in the shade. "Then what are we arguing about?" she purred, rising on her toes to brush her mouth against his.

That simple gesture ignited his libido faster than a match tossed in a can of gasoline. All the angst and misery that had started more than a week ago and gathered momentum until it reached flash point last night came together in a great wad of emotion that found its outlet in the kind of oblivion only she could offer.

The smooth, warm silk of her skin beneath his hands, the sweet, feminine pressure of her body against his most susceptible parts, the lure of her lips—what chance had logic to combat their potency? Even the straps of her skimpy little sundress fell under the spell she cast, obligingly slipping down past her shoulders to lay bare her breasts.

Leading her around the side of the rose arbor farthest from the house, he feasted his eyes on her loveliness, kissed her sun-dappled flesh and let his hands take a lazy detour down her long, supple spine.

"Ah…!" she sighed, angling her hips ever more intimately against him and almost destroying him. "I love it when you touch me like this. I love you…every part of you…here, and here, and—"

"Keep this up and we'll be doing it out here," he warned her hoarsely. "My stamina's not what it usually is."

"Oh, goodie," she gurgled, sending his blood pressure soaring to dangerous heights with her wicked explorations of his nether regions.

"This probably isn't a good idea, Julia," he said, in much the same tone of disapproving authority that Dopey likely used when he first discovered Snow White sleeping in his bed. "We both know we can't turn to sex to escape our problems."

"I'm not sure I subscribe to that theory," she said breathlessly, while her fingers played tag with the snaps of his fly. "In fact," she went on, sliding cool hands over his backside and leaving him standing there with his pants around his knees, "I think being intimate with the person you love…like this…can work miracles."

He was going to explode. The only question was, how soon?

Backing her against the convenient trunk of a nearby dogwood tree, he pushed her dress up around her waist and tugged at her underwear. Her panties slithered down around her ankles with a silken whisper. He touched her and knew he was not the only one in an advanced state of rampant desire. She was hot and sleek with wanting, the soft folds of her femininity already quivering with anticipation. And all for him!

She left him no time to gloat. Deftly, she closed her hand around him and guided him home.

''What will the neighbors think?'' he said against her mouth, and she gave a smothered gasp of laughter because she knew he was long past the point where he gave a rip about anything so mundane. Neighbors lining up six deep couldn't stop the vortex of passion ruling the moment.

It was only the second time they'd done it, but they came together as if they'd been practicing for years. Bracing his hands under her bottom, he held her to him and drove into her in one long sweep. Eyes wide, she let her head fall back, opened her mouth in a soundless exclamation and rocked against him.

''Slow down, sweetheart,'' he begged.

"I can't...!" she cried raggedly. "I... can't...."

Nor could he. She was contracting around him, pushing off the edge of reason and sending him soaring into sheer delirium. He heard a sound, something between a groan and a shout, followed by a soft answering cry, and felt her tears on his face.

Drained, he sank to the grass with her still wrapped around him. He was shaking all over, stripped of his strength and floundering to anchor himself to reality again. He thought his heart might flop out of his chest, it was thundering so hard and fast.

Gradually, the world swam back into focus. Above him, the roses swayed against the morning sky. Beside him, dew sparkled on the blades of grass. Against him, Julia lay warm and smelling sweetly of flowers and love. If he'd had his way, they could all have stayed like that through eternity. He'd never come so close to holding perfection in his grasp.

"Well?" Julia said, her voice as sultry as her glance. "Do you still want to talk about divorce?"

"As if you don't know the answer to that!" he said. "Cripes, was it my imagination, or did I let out one mother of a yell just at the crucial moment?"

"It wasn't your imagination," she said. "My grandmother probably heard you. Come to that, half the town probably heard you and sent someone to investigate. I can see the headlines now. Tourists Stunned by Bridegroom's Passionate Bellows!"

He rubbed his chin ruefully. "I was led astray. And I'd better not find a photo of my bare backside staring back at me from the front page of next week's edition of the local paper, or you're in trouble!"

"If my grandmother had come looking and found us in flagrante delicto, *you'd* have been the one in trouble." She gave him a sexy, complacent, utterly female smile. "I'd have told her you taught me everything I know."

He rolled her onto the grass and hauled his jeans back where they belonged. "On your feet, Mrs. Carreras, and make yourself decent before we hike back to the house. I don't want you ruining my image."

CHAPTER NINE

WHEN he came downstairs again, freshly shaved and showered, Felicity had the omelet pan warming on the stove. "I forgot to mention that I spoke to your mother this morning, Julia," she said, pouring in the egg mixture. "I was supposed to meet her and your father for brunch at the golf club, but when I explained what had happened to Michael, they understood why I canceled."

The mere mention of his in-laws was all Ben needed to ground him in reality again. "I can't imagine they were particularly interested in the news. They made it clear enough at the wedding that they weren't about to accept Michael into the family."

"Give them time, dear boy," Felicity said, adding slices of orange and a few grapes to the omelets she expertly shoveled onto plates. "They'll come around eventually."

"I doubt it. No disrespect to you, Felicity, but neither your son nor his wife strikes me as having your generosity of spirit." He shrugged. "But hey, it's their loss and I've got more important things to worry about than trying to convert them. Julia, are you planning to come with me to the hospital to see Michael?"

The look she directed at him across the table would have melted granite. "What do you think?" she said softly. "Of course I'm coming with you. He's my baby, too, remember?"

Why couldn't he just grab her words at face value and run with them? Why the uneasy feeling at the back of his mind that her capitulation had come about too quickly, too easily? "You don't have to do this all at once, sweetheart," he reminded her in a low voice not meant for Felicity's ears. "I'm happy with small steps taken one at a time."

"No. I meant what I said, out there in the garden."

He grinned. "You said quite a lot of things out there in the garden, ma'am! Which ones, exactly, are you referring to?"

Her face flamed. "The part about us being a family!" she said, slinging a furtive glance Felicity's way. "I want to honor *all* the vows I made in church, Ben, not just a select few."

"I guess that makes me one lucky guy, then."

If she meant what she said, that was—and she sounded adamant enough. Still, he couldn't shake a vague uneasiness that her words were prompted by a kind of *What other choice do I have if I want this marriage to hold together?* desperation. He'd taken a pretty hard line with her, after all.

"I really do mean it," she said, watching his face. "I love you, Ben. Being your wife is the most important thing in the world to me."

"And Michael?"

"I want what's best for him, which is why I've decided to hand in my notice at work. I want to be a full-time mother, not the sort who only sees her baby in the evenings and on weekends."

"I'd never ask you to give up your job, Julia," he said. "You love what you do and you've worked hard to get where you are. Not many women your age are marketing managers for a media company the size of McKinnon's.''

''My priorities have shifted. Writing copy for ad campaigns and researching target markets don't hold the same fascination anymore.''

He regarded her soberly. ''You do realize this is a hundred-and-eighty-degree turnaround from what you were saying a couple of weeks ago? You were all set then to accept another promotion.''

''Only because we hadn't planned to start a family right away. But now that we have...'' She lapsed into silence and let her smile complete the sentence.

She'd obviously convinced herself, so who was he to go around casting doubts? ''Okay. In that case, let's eat then hit the road. Felicity, would you like to come to the hospital with us? Not that I'm trying to get rid of you, you understand. You're welcome to stay here as long as you like.''

"Thank you, but I'll pass on both invitations this time," she said, taking the chair he pulled out for her. "Your little boy's got enough to deal with right now without a flock of strange faces hanging over him."

The huge balloon bouquet floating from the end of the crib in Michael's room, sent with love from Great-Amma Felicity, made Ben smile. The monstrously ostentatious flower arrangement on the dresser, with a card that read *Wishing you a speedy recovery, Stephanie and Garry Montgomery,* gave him gas.

"At least they sent *something,*" Julia said, seeing him wince. "And the colors do liven up the room."

Though there was doubtless some merit to her remarks, Ben would have been happy to toss the whole ghastly arrangement out of the window. But seeing Michael bright-eyed and alert disposed him to be generous. "I appreciate the gesture, honey," he said, and touched his forefinger to his son's cheek. "Hey,

Michael, you're looking pretty good, all things considered.''

''He knows your voice!'' On the other side of the crib, Julia was almost hopping with excitement. ''Look, Ben! He's smiling at you.''

He was! The little squirt was definitely baring his gums in a pint-size grin. ''Well, I'll be a monkey's uncle!'' Ben breathed, and wondered if it was normal for a father to get all choked over such a milestone.

The surgeon came in shortly after, with more good news. ''Your boy's a real trouper,'' he told them. ''At this rate, you'll be taking him home by the end of the week.''

For the next five days, Ben divided his time between the hospital and his downtown office, leaving the house early in the morning and not returning until evening, though he usually met Julia in the hospital cafeteria for a quick lunch.

But after the second day of holding dinner for him, she protested, ''I want to spend as much time with Michael as you do, Ben, but do you have to go to work as well? The only time I get to see you is when we're in bed.''

''It's the only time I get to see you, too,'' he said, leering at her. ''And may I say, I find the sight inspiring!''

''You know that's not what I mean. I hoped we could turn these few days that we're alone into a kind of mini-honeymoon.''

''Sweetheart,'' he said, taking her in his arms, ''the honeymoon's postponed, not canceled. As soon as things settle down, I'm taking you away to a private tropical island and lavishing you with attention, gourmet food, fine wines and the best sex you've ever dreamed of! Right now just isn't the time, though.''

''As if I don't know that! But since you'd already arranged to be away for a month after the wedding anyway, no one's expecting you to show up at work and take charge. So why do you have to be gone all day?''

''Because there's other business that needs taking care of and the time I'd be wasting traveling back and forth into town I'm using to attend to that.''

''Business to do with Marian, you mean?'' she said, and he was relieved to notice there was no hostility in her question.

''Kind of, yeah. Michael might have my DNA, but the night he was admitted to hospital brought home to me how few rights that gives me because I'm not the one named as his father on the birth certificate.''

''But they still let you give permission for his surgery.''

''Only because I bullied them into cutting through all the red tape with the threat of a major lawsuit if their nitpicking over petty details cost my son his life. Legally, I didn't have a leg to stand on and I can promise you, Julia, I don't ever intend to be put in that position again. By the time we bring that baby home, the custody and adoption applications are going to be in the works. God forbid it should ever happen, but the next time someone has to sign waivers on our son's behalf, that someone is going to be you or me.''

She chewed on that for a while, then, ''I hadn't looked at it that way, but you're absolutely right,'' she said, her frown clearing. ''Don't worry about me, Ben. I can keep myself occupied while you're looking after the legal end of things.''

''Occupied how? By going back to work, after all?'' He had to admit he wasn't too thrilled at the idea, for all that he'd said he'd never ask her to give up her job. The idea of leaving Michael with a nanny all day held little appeal.

''No,'' she said. ''I already told you I was going to resign, and I have. But there's still plenty to be done around here. We didn't anticipate having a baby in the house when we contracted for the renovations, and I intend to make up for that omission. By the time I'm done, this house is going to be a baby paradise.''

She was as good as her word. She fixed up the nursery, painting clouds and balloons on the ceiling, papering a frieze of rabbits along the top of the walls and hanging a colorful mobile above the crib.

She shopped for outfits, for stuffed toys, for CDs of nursery rhymes and lullabies. She bought a lamp that showed silhouettes of circus animals rotating in the base when the music box hidden underneath was wound up.

She bought a high chair.

"You're crazy," Ben said, sweeping her off her feet and planting her on the kitchen counter. "He's not going to fit into that thing for at least another six months."

"I want it there, ready and waiting for him when he does," she said.

She was wearing shorts and a sleeveless top. He ran his hands up her thighs and reveled in the flare of heavy-lidded passion in her eyes his touch produced. "But are you ready for me now?" he said huskily, knowing she was, and made love to her right there and then, fast and furiously because when he was locked inside her dark, sweet warmth, he always felt that nothing could ever again drive them apart.

She bought a playpen and a musical clown that rolled around under its own lopsided steam. "Seems to me you're having more fun with that thing than he ever will," Ben teased her, squatting beside her as she played with it.

They made love that time, too, though he did manage to contain himself long enough to haul her upstairs to their bed before stripping her naked and kissing every inch of delicious skin. Afterward, as they lay together in the afterglow of loving, he said, "You know, there's been a lot of hanky-panky going on around here in the last week, but we haven't talked about contraception. I know you went to see a doctor before we were married and were planning to go on the pill, but I've never asked…"

"I'm taking it," she said. "Most of the time, anyway."

"Most of the time?"

She curled up against him so that he couldn't see her face. "I did forget a couple of times, when Michael first got sick."

He could understand how that might happen. Between lack of sleep and worry, he'd been pretty punchy himself for a few days.

Another time, she bought a rocking chair, "Because," she said, when he playfully accused her of becoming a shopaholic, "I promised Michael I would, that night I stayed up with him and we really began to bond."

He could hardly argue with that. The chair was comfortable enough that even he could probably nap in it if he had to. And after the scare Michael had given them, Ben suspected it might be a long time before either he or Julia took for granted that any night-time fussiness was just part and parcel of a growing baby's normal development.

But he drew the line when he came home on Thursday, the day before Michael was due to be released from the hospital, to find that she'd bought a dog. "I wish you'd discussed it with me first," he said, regarding the mutt galloping over the lawn in the back garden. "Baby furniture and toys are one thing, but a dog...! Couldn't it have waited until things settled down a bit?"

"But Ben, we're creating an instant family, and pets are part of the picture."

She looked so crestfallen that he hadn't the heart to point out she could just as easily have settled for a goldfish. "Well, he's a handsome enough hound, I guess."

"And very good with small children."

Privately, Ben didn't plan on putting that claim to the test. Michael would be no more than a passing snack for a hungry beast the size of this one. "Where'd you find him?" he said, instead.

"At the local animal shelter. The people who owned him were apparently heartbroken at having to get rid of him."

Uh-huh! "So what did he do to persuade them to dump him at the pound? Swallow Grandma whole?"

"Oh, Ben!" She fondled the dog's ears, at which the benighted creature flopped over onto its back to show what a fine male specimen it was. "They're moving overseas, which would mean putting him in quarantine for six months, and they couldn't bear to do that to him. He's used to being around people and running free in a big garden. He'd be miserable locked up in a pen all day.''

He could think of a dozen arguments to counteract her reasons, but how could he oppose her after everything he'd already asked of her? And in all fairness, the mutt seemed gentle enough.

Smart, too! As if it knew its future hung in the balance, it parked itself at Ben's feet, one mother of a doggy grin on its face, but then got distracted and dug its paw about eight inches into its left ear.

''Does it have fleas?'' Ben said suspiciously.

''Certainly not!'' Julia jabbed an elbow in his ribs. ''Why would you even ask such a thing?''

''Because the farm dogs I grew up with used to scratch like that all the time and they were infested with the damn things. It was one of the reasons they weren't ever let into the house.''

''He's not a farm dog, he's a family dog, and thoroughly well-behaved.''

"Uh-huh." He eyed the mutt who ogled him back and thumped a lovelorn tail. "Does he have a name?"

"Of course. The children at his other home called him Clifford."

Cripes! Who in his right mind would stick a dog with a name like that? "It should be Oscar," he said, when the dog lifted a gentlemanly let's-get-acquainted paw. "He's putting on one hell of a good performance!"

"Then we can keep him and you'll let him live in the house?"

Didn't she know that when she gazed at him that way, he'd have let her keep a boa constrictor in the bathtub?

"Sure," he said. "We can keep him."

"Oh, Ben!" She flung her arms around his neck and nuzzled up against him in a way that she knew damned well would get him all in a lather. "I do love you!"

"Yeah, well, same here, and I'm more than ready to prove it," he said, dragging her toward the house, "but not with old Clifford panting on the sidelines!"

*   *   *

On the Sunday afternoon, the in-laws showed up. "We understand the child has been released from the hospital and felt we should at least stop by," Stephanie announced, obviously of the opinion she was doing them a favor they could never hope to repay. "Julia, darling, you look completely worn out. When does your husband propose to hire someone to take charge of his boy?"

"My boy," Ben said, forcing himself to adopt a reasonably civil tone, "is called Michael."

"Really?" Stephanie raised her immaculately mowed eyebrows. "Is that a family name, Benjamin?"

"No."

She allowed herself a malicious little smirk. "Perhaps on his mother's side, then?"

"You tell me, Stephanie," he said, smirking right back. "If anyone knows the Montgomery family tree by heart, I'm sure it's you."

She clapped her mouth shut so fast on that comeback, she could have given lessons to a snapping turtle. Face all pinched with annoyance, she cast a critical eye around the kitchen. "Is this one of your designs?"

"Yes. Would you like to commission one like it for your place?"

She shuddered delicately. "I *don't* think so!"

"Just as well," he said. "You'd have to wait at least a year before I could spare a crew to take on the job."

"Let me show you the rest of the house, Mother," Julia said, flinging him a pleading glance.

He shrugged apologetically. The old bat was enough to drive a man to drink, but she was Julia's mother and in her own warped, controlling way, she loved her daughter.

After the women left, Julia's father cleared his throat and said, "Sometimes my wife puts people's backs up without meaning to. She's actually very shy, you see."

Your wife is a living bitch! Ben thought. But there was no point in saying so. He had only to look at Garry Montgomery to know the man had been molded so firmly to the underside of

Stephanie's designer heel that the spirit had been stamped out of him years ago. The greater mystery was how Felicity had managed to produce such a spineless offspring in the first place.

"How is your son?" Garry went on, clearly unnerved by the lack of social small talk. "Is he going to be able to lead a…normal life— when he grows up, that is?"

"Yes, Garry," Ben said, maintaining a serious front with difficulty. "They didn't lop off his future manhood, if that's what you mean. The valve leading from his stomach was too narrow for food to pass through to the small intestine, that's all. It's not that uncommon a condition—one in every two hundred babies has it—and it can be corrected surgically without any other functions being jeopardized. The most Michael will have to put up with when he's of the right age is having some amorous young woman examining his scar and wanting to know how he got it."

The old man rolled a nervous eye in the direction his wife had taken. "Aarumph-heh!"

he said, letting rip with something between a cough and a guffaw.

Ben grinned and jerked a thumb at the refrigerator. "How about a beer while we're waiting for the women?"

"I haven't had a beer in years," Garry said. "Stephanie never keeps it in the house."

"We'll sneak outside with it, then. It's too nice a day to be indoors anyway and our dog could use the company."

Stephanie found them about ten minutes later. "We must be going, Garry," she declared, warding off Clifford who, apparently unable to tell the difference between her leg and a fire hydrant, was sniffing around her with scatalogical intent.

"I haven't finished my beer yet," Garry said, "and I wouldn't mind being given the grand tour. Unlike you, my dear, I like what Ben's done in the kitchen and I'm quite looking forward to seeing the rest of the house."

If he'd jumped up and bitten her in the face, Stephanie couldn't have looked more stunned. "You'll have to wait until another time," she said, separating each word into cast iron syllables. "The child is squalling and Julia is trying to calm him, though why it should fall to her to take care of his needs escapes me."

"Julia likes looking after him," Ben said lazily. "We both do. Parenthood agrees with us."

She bared her teeth in a chilling smile. "How nice. Come along, Garry."

Defeated, Garry put down his beer bottle and followed her through the garden to the car. "I'll show you around the next time you come out," Ben said, feeling sorry for the man even though he was the instrument of his own misery. "And if I didn't say so before, I do appreciate the flowers you sent to the hospital."

"Yes, well..." Stephanie took one last disparaging look at the facade of the house and drew in a deep cleansing breath. "If this really is what you and Julia want, I'm sure I wish you well."

Wish us well, my hind foot! Ben thought. *What you really mean is you'd like to stuff me and my bastard child headfirst down the nearest well!*

She didn't realize she'd fallen into a doze until Ben touched her shoulder. ''Hey,'' he said, ''I wondered what was keeping you. Why don't I take over in here and you go take a nap?''

''It's this chair,'' she said, smothering a yawn. ''It's *too* comfortable.''

''I think it's more that you're not getting enough rest. I hate to say it, but your mother's right. You do look worn out, honey.''

''I'm fine,'' she said, warmed by his concern. ''And I love rocking Michael to sleep. Are my parents still here?''

He shook his head. ''They left about ten minutes ago.''

She sighed. ''Good!''

''I thought you'd be glad to see them. I certainly never thought they'd drive all the way out here just to find out how Michael was doing.''

''Nice try, sweetheart,'' she said, shifting the baby to her other shoulder, ''but we both know that's not what prompted my mother to give up her Sunday afternoon golf game. She was hoping to find our marriage on the rocks and me ready to pack my bags and move back home. She pretty much came right out and asked how much longer I was prepared to put up with what I'd got myself into.''

Straddling the rocker, he trapped her knees between his legs. "And how long are you?"

"Forever!" she said vehemently. "And I let her know it in a way that left no room for misunderstanding. I'll *never* give her the satisfaction of saying 'I told you so!'''

He squatted in front of her and fixed her in one of his candid, far-seeing gazes. "If besting your mother's your only reason, Julia—"

"It's not," she whispered, hurt that he still suspected her motives after all they'd been through together. "I'm here because I love you, and I love Michael."

"I hope so," he said. "Because given the situation, I'm afraid you can't have one of us without the other."

"I know," she said, "and I wouldn't want it any other way."

"Okay," he said, so carefully that she knew he didn't entirely believe her.

"Why can't you accept that?" she pleaded. "What do I have to do to prove myself to you?"

"Maybe stop trying so hard," he said. "I think, over time, your dad will come to accept me. Stephanie, though, is a different matter altogether. We'll never see eye to eye. But she's still your mother, Julia, and I don't expect you to alienate yourself from her just to convince me that you're in this marriage for the long haul."

"What do you expect, then?" she cried, frustrated.

"That you take things one day at a time. Like I said before, small steps are okay, sweetheart. What matters is that you end up where you really want to be, and not where you think you ought to be."

"Then trust me to know the difference," she begged, "and remember my grandmother's advice. Don't go looking for problems that don't exist.''

She thought she'd finally gotten the message across because later that week, when he had to fly to a remote valley in the Interior, Ben's first thought was that he should take her and Michael with him.

''There's one of those fat farms up there,'' he said. ''You know the kind of place I mean, where rich women go to peel off the pounds.''

''Yes,'' she said, covering a smile. ''But I believe the polite term is 'health resort'.''

''I guess. Anyway, the owner wants to upgrade the place—put in state-of-the-art whirlpools and steam baths and outfit each suite with its own luxury bathroom, to attract the rich and famous. I'd send someone else but he's asked me to be there for the initial planning phase and this is too big a contract for me to turn down.''

''So go,'' she said. ''It'll only be for a few days and we'll be fine by ourselves.''

''But you could use a change of scene and it's beautiful up there at this time of year.''

"It's also very hot, Ben. Ninety degrees isn't uncommon."

"Yeah, but there's a good hotel in town, right on the lake, with an outdoor pool and nice gardens where you could relax." He cupped her breast possessively. "Come with me, Julia, and let's take that mini-honeymoon you were talking about the other week."

"But we'd hardly see you," she said, clinging to reason despite his shameless attempts at bribery. "You're going to be tied up all day, working on plans with the resort owner."

"I'd be with you at night, though. That's better than nothing."

It was, but not much, and in the end, she persuaded him to leave her and Michael at home. "Babies his age don't tolerate extreme heat very well, especially if they're not used to it," she pointed out. "And he's making such a good recovery that I'd hate to do anything that might bring on a relapse."

That proved the clinching argument. Ben left a couple of days later, alone. "I'll phone you every evening,'' he promised, giving her and Michael a hug.

''Hurry back,'' she said, a pang of loneliness already threatening.

He dropped a swift, hard kiss on her mouth. ''You know I will. The custody hearing comes up a week from Monday and I'm not about to miss that. Count on my being home that weekend, if not before.''

Of course, she missed him, especially at night when the only thing she had to curl up against was his pillow. But she enjoyed having the baby all to herself, too. She knew it was natural, given Michael's illness and the sorry circumstances surrounding his birth, that Ben should have immersed himself so thoroughly in the role of parent, but his doing so had exacerbated Julia's sense of being on the periphery of things; an accessory after the fact, rather than an essential part of the family unit.

With him gone, she felt for the first time like a real mother, and she loved every minute of it. What could be sweeter than the damp warmth of a sleeping baby's breath against one's neck? she wondered. What else filled a woman's heart to overflowing the way that wide, toothless baby smile did at the sight of his mother's face?

The days rolled by, full of sun and lazy hours in the garden; the nights were calm and peaceful. She wasn't nervous alone in the big house because Clifford appointed himself protector of the family the minute Ben left. He slept at the foot of her bed some of the time, and at others she found him in the nursery, next to the crib.

''Well, darling girl,'' her grandmother said, on one of her many visits, ''I'm proud of you and Ben! You've managed to do what few other couples could, and look how it's paying off. Michael is thriving beautifully and it's easy to see you're the light of his little life. He watches your every move.''

''I never knew I could love like this,'' Julia said, tears suddenly springing to her eyes. ''I adore him, Amma, and I don't know why I'm crying about it. I'm happier than I ever dreamed possible.''

In fact, she'd been crying a lot lately. Anything or nothing could get her going: the sunset, a perfect rose, the sight of Michael sleeping with his little fat fist tucked under his chin, Clifford racing down the stairs with a nursery toy stuffed in his mouth, the wedding portrait of her and Ben that stood on the dresser in their bedroom—all fair game.

The weepiness was the first in a series of clues that led her to suspect Michael might soon be sharing his nursery with a sister or brother, and when she took a home pregnancy test, all doubt was removed.

Missing a couple of days of birth control pills earlier in the month had been enough of an omission for a new life to get started.

CHAPTER TEN

BECAUSE Ben would be back on the Sunday, Julia decided to wait until then to tell him the news. She wasn't sure how he'd take it and confessed to being a little nervous. She'd wanted to start a baby as soon as they were married and he'd had a hard time dissuading her. Would he think she'd been deliberately careless, just to get her own way? Or worse, that she was retaliating because he'd left her no choice but to accept Michael?

She'd never thought that sharing the news that she was pregnant would give rise to anything less than complete and delirious joy, but too much had happened lately for her to believe that a wedding ring had the power to ward off trouble.

Marriage, even when two people were deeply in love, wasn't a guarantee of happy ever after; it was only as strong as the commitment and trust each party brought to it. Already, hers and Ben's had faltered badly. Adding yet another unexpected baby to the mix might prove fatal.

But her fears took second place to a much more threatening apprehension when the doorbell rang on Friday afternoon, and she found Marian Dawes standing on the front porch.

''I had to come,'' she said, before Julia could open her mouth. ''I know I don't have the right, but I had to see him one last time before I sign him over to you. Please don't send me away.''

Mutely, Julia opened the door wider and gestured her inside, too appalled by the woman's appearance to speak. Marian's pretty face was marred by a purple bruise on her cheek and her eyes were haunted.

She scuttled through the door as if the hounds of hell were chasing her. ''Thank you,'' she said. ''Thank you so much, Mrs. Carreras. I'm very grateful to you.''

Why, she's shaking! Julia realized and, moved to compassion, touched her gently on the arm. ''Have you been in an accident, Marian?''

''No...no!'' Instinctively, Marian put up a hand to hide her poor battered face. ''I bumped into my car door—clumsy of me, I know.''

Julia didn't believe her for a moment. ''Come into the kitchen and let me get you something to put on that bruise,'' she said, steering her down the hall toward the back of the house.

''I don't want to be any trouble. If I could just see my—*your* baby, I'll be on my way.''

''Michael's sleeping, but he should wake up shortly. You won't mind waiting, I'm sure, and it'll give me time to fix you something to drink. You look as if you need something to fortify you.''

In truth, she could use something herself! She felt sick inside. Sick and angry for Marian and, if she were honest, very afraid of her, too. That the woman was distraught was obvious, but it hardly explained her insistence on seeing Michael. Was she having a last-minute change of heart about giving him up?

"You know the custody hearing's all set for Monday, of course?" she said, folding crushed ice into a clean tea towel.

"Yes." Uncertainly, Marian hovered in the middle of the kitchen. "That's one reason I'm here, but I came a day or two earlier in the hope that I'd catch you at home and you'd let me see the baby one last time. I wasn't sure you'd bring him to the courthouse with you."

Somewhat reassured, Julia said, "Come and sit down, Marian, and hold this to your face. I'm going to make you a cup of tea, unless you'd prefer coffee or something cold?"

"Tea would be nice," she sighed, then said again, "but I don't want to be any trouble."

"It's no bother. I was going to make some for myself anyway. I've got into the habit of having a cup while I give Michael his afternoon bottle."

"Is he better, Mrs. Carreras—from the operation, I mean?"

"Yes, he's better," Julia said gently. "And Marian, won't you please call me Julia?"

"I don't have the right." The big blue eyes filled with tears. "I ruined your wedding day and probably your marriage, too. But I didn't know what else to do. Ben—" She gestured helplessly "—it had been over between us for months, but he was the only person I felt I could turn to. He's a decent, good man, Mrs. Carreras."

And you, Julia thought, her heart aching with pity, *though misguided and weak, are a good woman and deserve better than what you've settled for.* "How do you take your tea, Marian?" she said. "It's Earl Grey and I like mine with lemon."

"I'll have the same." She eyed the delicate cup and saucer Julia handed to her with almost fearful awe. "What pretty china. I can never keep anything like this at my house. It always gets broken."

I just bet it does! Julia thought, her anger surging up afresh. "Wayne did that to you, didn't he?" she said, indicating the bruise.

Marian almost dropped her cup in shock. "Why would you think that?" she gasped. "I told you, I walked into my car door."

"A woman who accidentally walks into her car door doesn't look frightened to death all the time. She doesn't flinch at every little noise." She waited for another denial, and when it didn't come, said quietly, "Does he beat you up often, Marian?"

For a moment, Marian's stare was that of a terrified deer caught in the headlights, then, "Not often, no," she said, and began to cry again. "And when he does, it's usually my fault. I provoke him."

Was it early pregnancy that made the tea rise up in her throat, Julia wondered, or disgust? "And did Michael provoke him, too? Is that how he happened to have a bruise on his arm when you brought him to us?"

"Wayne never hit the baby!" Marian insisted. "It was just that Junior cried a lot and kept throwing up. It got on Wayne's nerves and he sometimes got a bit rough trying to make him be quiet."

Oh, God! Julia pressed a hand to her mouth to still its trembling and stood up. She needed to hold Michael close to her heart, to kiss his little head and tell him that she and his daddy loved him and would never let anyone hurt him again.

"I think I hear the baby," she said, when she could control her voice. "Help yourself to more tea if you like, while I go to get him."

Marian was sitting on the back doorstep, stroking Clifford, but when she heard Julia come back to the kitchen with Michael, she sprang to her feet.

"Well, here he is," Julia said, desperately trying not to show how terrified she was by the avid look in Marian's eyes as she gazed down at the child she'd given birth to and then, so soon after, given away.

"Oh, Mrs. Carreras, he's beautiful!"

"Thank you. We think so, too."

"He has his father's blue eyes but he's dark-haired like both of you."

"Yes."

There was something distinctly odd about such a conversation. Had she wandered into Alice's Wonderland by mistake, Julia wondered, that they were both behaving as if she, and not Marian, was the birth mother?

"Can I...would you let me hold him?"

The unspoken fear clutched at Julia again. Instinctively, she hugged Michael closer.

"Just for a minute? Please?" Marian held out her arms pleadingly. "I won't drop him or hurt him."

What would Ben have done, had he been there?

Marian's basically decent...she's trying to make up for her mistakes, he'd once said. *She's not inherently vicious...she'll always be Michael's birth mother but she gave him to us because she wanted what was best for him....*

The answer was clear enough. If Marian could show such unselfish generosity, the least Julia could do was return the favor. "Here," she said, placing the baby in her arms. "Why don't we sit outside and you can give him his bottle?"

"You'd let me do that?" Marian's voice was hushed, her expression awed, as if kind-

ness was the last thing she expected from anyone.

Should she? Was she being magnanimous,
or merely a fool?

The question nagged at Julia while she
warmed the formula and refilled the teapot.
She could see Marian beyond the French
doors, sitting at the table in the shade of the
patio umbrella and singing softly to Michael.
What if, while Julia's back was turned, she
made a sudden dash for her car and drove off
with him? What if holding him again rece-
mented the powerful bond between birth
mother and child. Blood was thicker than water, after all.

Julia hadn't thought much about her own
pregnancy, but she knew at the moment that
nothing could ever induce her to part with the
baby she was carrying. Could Marian be so
very different?

Panicked, she piled everything on a tray and
raced outside to discover something that hadn't
been apparent from her standpoint in the
kitchen. Clifford lay stretched out about six

feet away from Marian, his head on his paws, his eyes tracking her every movement.

Breathing a quiet sigh of relief, Julia bent to fondle his ears. How could she have forgotten Clifford, their self-appointed guard dog? If Marian were to try to bolt the scene, she wouldn't get very far. Clifford would see to that.

But Marian was too engrossed with feeding Michael to have thoughts for anything else, and for the next while, the only sounds disturbing the silence were the faint sea breeze ruffling the leaves of the dogwood tree and Michael's little grunts of satisfaction as he downed the milk.

''Look how he loves you, Mrs. Carreras,'' she said, turning him so that he was facing Julia when he'd finished. ''He never takes his eyes off you for a minute. He knows who his mommy is, that's for sure.''

''I think,'' Julia replied unsteadily, ''that's the nicest thing anyone could say to me but for you to be the one, Marian…!'' She swallowed. ''I can't begin to tell you how moved I am.''

Fortunately, Michael eased the emotional tension of the moment by letting out a resounding burp. Marian sat him on her lap and if she didn't quite laugh out loud, she at least managed a real smile. Unimpressed, the baby wriggled in her arms, looking for Julia and breaking into an endearing gummy grin when he found her.

"Well, I guess I've got what I came for," Marian said, handing him over to her. "Thank you for being so kind, Mrs. Carreras. Now that I know for sure I made the right decision and that he's in such good hands, I can go."

An hour ago, Julia would have welcomed the idea. She'd have thought even allowing the woman inside the house was above and beyond the call of duty. But suddenly, what she'd done didn't strike her as nearly enough.

"No," she said, spreading a blanket on the grass and laying Michael down on it so that he could kick his little legs and gurgle at the leaves shimmering against the sky. "Please stay a while longer. We're women, Marian, and women can talk to each other in a way that men don't seem able to do. And I can't let you walk out of here without urging you to try to find your way to a better life.''

''I've got a good enough life,'' Marian said, the scared uneasy shadows returning to her eyes.

''How can that be? Wayne Dawes is a bully.''

''He's my husband, Mrs. Carreras. I love him.''

''He's a monster,'' Julia said determinedly. ''He hit you, and if you hadn't brought Michael to us when you did, he'd have hit him by now. How can you love a man like that? Leave him, Marian, before he hurts you really badly.''

Before he kills you is what she wanted to say, but the woman was deaf to persuasion.

''I can't,'' she whispered. ''I need him. It's not as if he's a bad man. After all, he forgave me for cheating on him with Ben and let me come home again. It wouldn't be fair for me to walk out on him again, just because he lost his temper with me.''

Julia ground her teeth in frustration. "He isn't worth what he's costing you, don't you see that? And it's not too late for you to start over again. You're young, you're pretty, you're smart. There are people who'll help you. Please, Marian! When Michael asks when you're coming to visit, I don't want to have to tell him that you can't, because your husband beat you up and put you in a body cast."

"I won't be coming to see Michael anyway. He's not my child anymore."

"He might be living with us, but in the most basic sense Michael will always be your child. I didn't want to acknowledge that at first, but I know now that it's true." She touched her still slender waist. "I'm pregnant and even though it's early days yet and I don't look any different, I already know nothing can ever sever a mother's blood tie with her baby. So if you won't make a change for your own sake, Marian, do it for Michael's. Make him proud of you. Don't let him grow up thinking you traded him for a man like Wayne Dawes."

"I'll think about it," she said, but the long defeated sigh accompanying her words told Julia she wouldn't. Wayne Dawes had done a good job convincing her that the abuse he heaped on her was no less than she deserved. "I've got to go now. Wayne's waiting at the motel and he'll get mad if I'm late. I guess," she said, offering to shake hands, "I'll see you in court on Monday?"

"Yes." Julia did something then that she'd never have envisaged herself ever doing. She put her arms around Marian's thin shoulders and hugged her. "But if you ever need help…"

For a moment, Marian clung to her like a lost child, then stepped away and said, "I'll be okay. Wayne and I might fight sometimes, but we always make up."

She bent to touch Michael one last time, but backed away quickly at Clifford's low growl. "Take care, little guy," she said in a choked voice. "You don't know how lucky you are."

Close to tears herself, Julia took her arm. "Come on, I'll walk you to your car."

* . * *

Fists clenched, Ben remained hidden in the kitchen and waited until he heard the side gate clang shut before stepping out into the garden to rescue Michael.

To think he'd rushed home two days early, just to be with his wife! His beautiful, conniving, manipulative wife, who'd seized the first chance she got to sabotage his efforts to gain legal custody of his son! He hadn't heard everything she'd been saying to Marian, but he'd caught enough to get the gist of the conversation.

Oh, a fine mother she was, so busy dishing out self-serving advice that she didn't care one whit that the child she professed to love could be mauled to death while her back was turned! Her great hairy beast of a dog was practically lying on top of Michael who'd managed to grab a fistful of its mangy fur and was trying to stuff it in his mouth.

''Out of the way, dog,'' Ben practically snarled, scooping the baby into his arms.

He scarcely made it inside the French doors before Julia came haring back along the side path, took one look at the dog and the rumpled blanket where the baby was supposed to be, and went into a fit of shrieking hysterics.

"Something wrong, darling?" Ben inquired, stepping out of the shadowed breakfast room and into the sunlight.

She spun to face him and for a moment he almost felt sorry for her. Her face was the color of putty, her eyes blank with shock and her chest heaving. When she saw he had Michael in his arms, she went so limp with relief that he thought she was going to faint.

She recovered, though. Pressing her hand to her heart—or the place he'd always assumed it was supposed to be—she fell into the nearest patio chair. "My heavens, you scared me, Ben!"

Good! he thought. "Sorry, *darling,*" he said. "I thought you'd be glad to see me home again. If I'd known it was going to cause you such distress, *darling,* I'd have stayed away a bit longer."

She seemed to realize then that all was not well in paradise. Those atypical darlings he was throwing around, his too-smooth tone of voice and the fact that he wasn't acting like a damned fool and slobbering kisses all over her, finally penetrated the fog of panic that had briefly possessed her.

"What's the matter?" she said. "Why are you looking at me like that?"

"How would you like me to look at you, Julia?" he returned coldly.

Warily, she got to her feet and leaned against the patio table. "As if you're as glad to see me as I am to see you, instead of as if you were confronting a stranger."

"But I am," he said. "You're not who I thought you were."

"Ben!" She came toward him, every soft, deceiving feminine wile on full alert. "You're not making any sense. I'm your wife, and I love you."

"Yes," he said, tossing the words over his shoulder and returning to the house. "I suppose in your own warped way, you do. I suppose you think that justifies stabbing me in the back."

"I have done no such thing!" she exclaimed vehemently.

Such righteous indignation was enough to set his own anger boiling over. "Oh, can the act, Julia!" he snapped, spinning to confront her. "I witnessed your touching little scene with Marian. I know what you're up to."

"Then explain it to me," she shot back, "because I obviously missed something! Exactly what do you think you saw and heard?"

"Enough. I'm not stupid, Julia, though I'm beginning to think you must be, to leave a baby unattended around a great slobbering dog."

"Oh, baby, what happened?" Face mirroring commendable concern, she went to take Michael from him. "Did that big old Clifford scare you?"

"If it didn't, it's no thanks to you!" Ben said savagely. "Michael's no better off in your care than he was in Marian's!"

"That's unfair, Ben! To me and to Marian!"

"Oh, really?" he sneered. "And when did you and she become such bosom buddies?"

She looked at him then the way her mother usually looked at her father: as if he weren't playing with a full deck and needed someone to lead him around by the hand and take charge of his life. "I can't imagine why you're asking me that, since you seem to think you have the answers to everything. But you're right on one score. Any explanations you feel you're entitled to can wait until I've looked after Michael. Stop hanging on to him as if you think I might kidnap him and let me take him up to the nursery and change his diaper."

"No," he said. "He's my son and I'll do it."

"I thought he was my son, too."

"Yeah, well, we all make mistakes, Julia. Some of us more than others."

She lifted her elegant shoulders in mystified surrender. "Go look after the baby," she said in a saintly voice, "then you and I had better sit down and talk like rational adults."

"Rational adults, my ass!" he fairly bel-lowed. "We'll lay everything out on the table, all right, but you can forget the polite society small talk! When I'm faced with a down and dirty fighter, I retaliate in like fashion. And you, *my darling,* are one down and dirty fighter!"

When he came back downstairs with Michael fifteen minutes later, he found her sitting at the table in the breakfast room, spine as straight as a yardstick, and staring out at the ocean with her face frozen in a kind of distant calm. The dog lay at her feet.

"How is Michael?" she said politely, not deigning to look at him.

"Okay, considering."

"Considering what? He wasn't alone for more than a couple of minutes."

"A couple of minutes is all it takes, Julia," he said, resenting the flicker of guilt stirring inside him. "How you could even think it was okay to leave a helpless little kid with a big dog like that escapes me."

''If you're suggesting I'm an unfit mother—''

''That's exactly what I'm suggesting, sweetheart. I thought I could trust you to care for my son, yet the first time I leave you in charge, this is what happens to him. And that's only the half of it. What the hell were you doing, encouraging Marian to walk out on Wayne and take Michael back again? I thought you were on my side, Julia.''

''Where ever did you get such an idea?'' she cried, her face paling.

''By listening in on your sickeningly sympathetic conversation. They do say eavesdroppers never hear good of themselves, but I have to admit, I hadn't bargained on your betraying me quite so thoroughly.''

''That's insane! Nothing about our conversation could be construed as disloyal to you.''

''Oh?'' He parked Michael in his swing, planted both hands flat on the table and recited, ''Michael will always be your child... Nothing can ever destroy a mother's connection with her baby... Don't let him grow up knowing you traded him for a man like Wayne Dawes.... Does any of that ring a bell, Julia? Have you got the nerve to sit there and deny you said those things to Marian?''

''No,'' she said defiantly. ''I said all that, and more, but you're obviously not nearly as smart as you'd like to think you are, or you'd have listened to all the things I said instead of a select few. You'd know, for instance, that I'm pregnant.''

Trying not to let her see how that rocked him, he straightened up and raked his glance over her. ''Well, of course you are, honey. It's what you've been after all along, after all, hasn't it? And you always get what you want, don't you, regardless of any agreement we might have reached to the contrary? No wonder you're so anxious to be rid of Michael. He's served his purpose now. You don't need him to fulfill your maternal yearnings any more, do you?''

She stood up then and traded him glare for glare. ''Listen to me, you arrogant, pigheaded fool! I was not talking Marian into reclaiming your son, I was encouraging her to walk away from her rotten husband before he breaks every bone in her body. I was repeating what you've been preaching all along and, for the first time since this whole mess of a marriage started, I truly believed what I was saying.''

''You don't give a rat's ass about Marian. All you care about is getting rid of her son to make way for your baby.''

''Your baby, too, Ben, or are you going to suggest you're not the father?'' She puffed out a little breath of disgust. ''You once said that Marian is the victim in this whole situation and you were right. It's not you and not me, and not, thank God, that little boy over there. She came here for one last visit with her son because she thought that once she signed him over to us, she'd never see him again. But I told her she didn't have to worry because no matter who was looking after him, *she* was his natural mother and was welcome to see him whenever she wanted to. And while you might be sorry that I'm pregnant, I'm not. Because...'' She folded her hands over her stomach, and her voice, which had started out full of fire, broke as she continued, ''It's taken this new life growing inside me for me to realize what a precious gift a child is and I wouldn't deny *anyone* the right to that.''

She made him feel about as sensitive as a rogue elephant on the rampage. ''Oh, Julia…!''

''Shut up!'' she spat. ''I'm not finished. I begged Marian to leave her husband because he's a bully and a brute. Well, the way you've acted since you got home today, Ben Carreras, you're not a whole lot better!''

He slumped down onto his chair again and dropped his head in his hands. ''I'm sorry! I know that doesn't exactly cut it, but I don't know what else to say. My only excuse is that what I saw and heard scared me spitless, and the rest just…came spilling out.''

She didn't answer right away. Instead she loaded cups into the dishwasher.

Eventually, she said, ''It's not all your fault. I shouldn't have left Michael alone, and you're right about the dog. He's too big to be let loose around such a little baby. But they're only symptoms of a much deeper problem, Ben. The real issue is you and I are both constantly looking for slights and betrayal where none are intended. We're so busy worrying about what the other's trying to take away that we don't see what each has to give. I can't speak for you, but I know I need to figure out how to repair the damage before it's too late.''

CHAPTER ELEVEN

SHE picked up her purse then, and took out her car keys.

"And is this how you propose we go about it—by running out on me again?" he blustered, refusing to admit to himself how terrified he was by the realization that this time, he'd given her good reason not to come back. "Because let me tell you, now that you're carrying my child, you no longer have that option. You'll damned well stay here with me and that's all there is to it!"

She looked at him as if he'd just crawled out from under a rock. "That's probably exactly how Wayne Dawes speaks to Marian," she said dully. "The difference is, while she's prepared to tolerate it, I'm not."

If she'd hauled off and decked him, he couldn't have been more shocked. *Him a car-*

bon copy of Wayne Dawes? "For crying out loud, Julia, you can't be serious!"

She bit her lip and sighed. "No, I don't suppose I am. But your ongoing suspicion of my every motive is beginning to wear me down. You sneak around listening in on half a conversation and decide I'm conspiring against you. I say I want to spend some time figuring out what I can do to make this marriage work, and you immediately assume I'm leaving you."

"Well, it wouldn't be the first time you just disappeared."

"But I've always come home again and the reason is exactly the same as the one that's guided me to every other decision I've made regarding us and our marriage over the last few weeks. I love you. I'm beginning to see, though, that just saying so isn't enough. It's what a person's prepared to do to prove it that counts and I guess I just haven't given you enough reasons to believe me."

She felled him with that parting shot and though his first instinct was to go after her and beg her to stay, he was too ashamed. He'd asked more of her than any husband had the right to ask. He'd taken her new-bride dreams and trampled them in the dust of a shabby affair that never should have happened. He'd faced her with one ultimatum after another and she'd conceded to him every time. He'd smeared the news of her pregnancy with insult, even though he knew having a baby had been the thing she wanted more than anything else.

He needed to have his butt kicked. Hell, he needed a lobotomy!

Michael was fed, bathed and asleep for the night before she came home again. It was dusk by then, and Ben was sitting in the library, the way he had the first time she disappeared on him, and even though the house was full of evening shadows when she came in through the front door, he saw at once that she'd been crying. Her eyes were red and puffy and if it was possible for her ever to look anything other than stunningly beautiful, she looked it then.

If there were words to cover the situation, he'd never heard of them. There was absolutely nothing he could say to erase the hurt he'd dealt her. So he did the only other thing at his disposal and prayed it would be enough. He went to her and took her in his arms.

She didn't rebuff him, but then what reason had she ever given him to think she would? She'd loved him from the day they'd met but because he was a fool, he hadn't believed she was just as beautiful on the inside as she was on the outside.

He'd waited for the inevitable ax to fall, the way it so often had when he was growing up. Waited for her to decide she didn't want him around anymore and just to make sure she didn't disappoint him, he'd given her every reason to walk away. Instead, she kept coming back for more.

To his horror, he started to cry, great rib-shaking sobs that rocked him to the soles of his feet. Big, thick-as-a-brick jerk that he was, he stood there bawling like a kid, dripping

tears all over her hair and making idiotic glug-
ging noises as if he were choking.

She just wrapped her arms around his waist
and held on, the way she always did. ''Thank
you,'' he croaked, when he finally pulled himself together enough to articulate the words.
''Thank you for not giving up on us.''

Still, she didn't speak. She just pressed her
face into his shoulder and the next thing, they
were heading up to the bedroom. He hadn't
eaten dinner and he didn't think she had, either, but it wasn't food they needed to restore
them, it was each other.

The onshore breeze wafted the scent of
flowers and summer through the open windows. He sank with her to the cool, smooth
sheets, holding her close the whole time because he couldn't bear to see the bruised hurting in her eyes.

The loving came slowly. A kiss that landed
at the corner of her lips and slid to her mouth
with quiet, desperate need. A touch to her face,
and then her throat, and then her shoulder;

flowing like the tide, quietly, secretively almost.

When at last he entered her, she received him warmly, embracing him with all the generosity that was her trademark. Locked in her arms, he let the climax roll over him, slow sweet agony that he wished would never end. Loving had never been like that before. Never so reverent. And somehow never so sad.

''When did you last eat?'' he asked her, suddenly afraid.

She lay beside him, her eyes closed. ''I don't remember.''

''Sweetheart,'' he said, ''you're pregnant. You need to take care of yourself, of our baby.''

''I know.'' She went to get out of bed, her movements listless and once again he caught the gleam of tears in her eyes. ''I'm going to check on Michael.''

''No,'' he said, tucking the covers around her shoulder. ''You stay put and let me do it. Then I'll fix you a snack before you go to sleep.''

He made sandwiches and hot chocolate, then went looking for the dog, only to find it had gone missing. *Oh, jeez, Clifford!* he thought, scanning the path that led from the garden down to the beach. *This is one hell of a time to pull a disappearing act!*

He half-hoped Julia would have fallen asleep when he went back upstairs, but she was wide awake. "Honey," he said carefully, laying the tray on her bedside table, "I don't want to alarm you, but I can't find Clifford. I figure he got out somehow and made tracks for the beach, so I'm going to—"

"He's not lost," she said, one fat tear rolling down her face. "I took him back to the shelter."

"You *what?*"

"I took him back."

"But you loved that crazy mutt!"

"He might hurt Michael."

So this was what a worm felt like: lower than dirt and just about as unappealing! "Julia," he said, "Clifford doesn't have a mean bone in his body, and I know it. You didn't have to do this.''

''Yes, I did,'' she said.

''Oh, *hell!*'' He wiped a despairing hand over his face. He wasn't fit to look after a loaf of bread, let alone a baby. As for being a husband…a fruit fly could do a better job!

''Come to bed,'' she said, patting his hand. ''What's done is done, and they promised me at the shelter they'd make sure Clifford goes to a good home.''

She slept late the next morning, an amazing feat, given that there was a baby in the house. When she awoke, she found a thermos of tea and a plate of crackers beside the bed—and a note.

Hi, sweetheart! it read. *Don't know if you're having morning sickness but I once read somewhere that crackers and tea help prevent it, so thought I'd leave you prepared. Michael and I have gone for a walk along the seawall, but we'll be back in time to take you out for lunch.*

In fact, she did feel sick. Sick and miserable, if truth be told, but it had nothing to do with her being pregnant. She'd put on the best face she could last night, but the business with Clifford...

Oh, she'd loved him! Loved how he'd appointed himself in charge when Ben was away. Loved how gentle and faithful he was, how careful around the baby. She'd had such hopes, imagining the two of them when Michael was bigger: a boy and his dog wading in the warm shallow pools when the tide was out, chasing a ball on the sand flats...the kind of closeness with a pet she'd wanted when she was a child, but had never been allowed to have.

Silly of her, no doubt, to let herself get so upset about a dog she hadn't even known existed a month ago, but she just couldn't shake the way Clifford had looked back at her as he was being led away to the holding pen at the animal shelter. As if she'd just cut his throat. As if he was being led to the slaughterhouse.

Closing her eyes to stem the tears, she leaned back against the pillows. Instead of wallowing in self-pity, she'd be better off counting her blessings. She and Ben had weathered more storms in a few weeks of marriage than most people had to cope with in a lifetime. There'd been pain and heartache along the way, but their love had strengthened from it.

They had each other, they had Michael, and they had another baby on the way. Most people would say they were rich beyond deserving. Some would say losing a dog didn't merit a mention. If only she could believe that...

Downstairs, a door slammed and she heard footsteps on the stairs. Shortly after, Ben appeared with Michael in his arms. ''Hey, Mommy, you awake?''

She opened her eyes and smiled determinedly. ''I'm awake.''

''Good,'' he said, ''because there's someone here who's very anxious to see you.''

''Well, let me have him then! I've missed him.''

''From all accounts, the feeling was mutual,'' Ben said, and opened the door wider.

Expecting he'd simply bring Michael to her, she held out her arms and crooned, "Come here, my baby."

Instead, Clifford came bounding into the room, leaped on the bed and with manic ecstasy, proceeded to wash as much of her as he could get at, which was plenty since she hadn't a stitch on under the sheets.

"Oh, Ben!" she exclaimed, smiling and laughing and crying all at the same time. "You didn't have to do this."

"Yes, I did," he said soberly, wrestling Clifford aside so that all four of them could fit on the bed. "It's taken me a while to realize it, but I've done a lot of taking since we exchanged our wedding vows and I figure it's about time I did a little giving for a change. And to quote a lovely lady I know rather well, how else do I prove that I'm committed to you and our marriage?"

She batted her eyelashes at him. "I could think of a couple of other ways, if you insist on being noble."

"So can I," he said, with an outrageously lascivious wink. "But if it's all the same to you, I'll take a number and stand in line. Michael's too young to be taking lessons in the art of seduction and I don't care to share your favors with a dog, even if he is one of the family."

Heart overflowing, she said, "Do you know how much I love you, Ben Carreras?"

"I'm beginning to get the picture," he said, planting a kiss on her mouth. "Do you know how proud I am to be your husband, and how glad I am that you're the mother of both my children?"

MILLS & BOON® PUBLISH EIGHT LARGE PRINT TITLES A MONTH. THESE ARE THE EIGHT TITLES FOR SEPTEMBER 2000

THE SHEIKH'S REWARD
Lucy Gordon

HER SECRET PREGNANCY
Sharon Kendrick

MARRIAGE IN PERIL
Miranda Lee

BRIDE ON LOAN
Leigh Michaels

THE MISTRESS DECEPTION
Susan Napier

THE UNEXPECTED WEDDING GIFT
Catherine Spencer

A WIFE AT KIMBARA
Margaret Way

A SCANDALOUS ENGAGEMENT
Cathy Williams

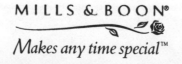

MILLS & BOON®

Makes any time special™

MILLS & BOON® PUBLISH EIGHT LARGE PRINT TITLES A MONTH. THESE ARE THE EIGHT TITLES FOR OCTOBER 2000

─────── ❧ ───────

JUST SAY YES!
Caroline Anderson

THE PERFECT FATHER
Penny Jordan

THE CATTLE KING'S MISTRESS
Emma Darcy

TO MARRY A SHEIKH
Day Leclaire

THE ITALIAN SEDUCTION
Mary Lyons

A MOTHER FOR MOLLIE
Barbara McMahon

BOUND BY CONTRACT
Carole Mortimer

A MISTRESS WORTH MARRYING
Kay Thorpe

MILLS & BOON®
Makes any time special™